The Tenacious Goldbrick

In This Series

The Margarita Solution

Chiseler with a Glass Jaw

When the Contralto Sings

Stalking the Scratch Man

The Tenacious Goldbrick

Cryptic Paisley

The Tenacious Goldbrick

The Tenacious Goldbrick

Chester Henry

DAGMAR
MIURA
LOS ANGELES

Published by Dagmar Miura
Los Angeles
www.dagmarmiura.com

The Tenacious Goldbrick

First published 2021

ISBN: 978-1-951130-57-2

ONE

AT THE TOP OF Laurel Canyon, just past the stoplight at Mulholland, Celeste pulled out of the traffic, onto the verge, and clicked on the dome light, taking a moment to dig around in the console. She was after a pill that she knew was in there, a little white Ritalin tab that would serve as a pick-me-up. In the darkness, with the headlights streaming by on the left, she didn't even see the guy until he yanked open the passenger door.

Wearing a leather biker jacket and jeans, he hopped in and pulled the door closed, then reached up to click off the dome light, rattling off a rapid string of Spanish. The only thing she could pick out was *señora*, a word that people used when they spoke to her mother.

"Get out of my car," Celeste said, raising her voice as she overcame her surprise.

"Can you give me a ride?" He slouched in the seat and turned to look out the side window. "Please—it's a matter of life and death."

"Are you running from the cops?"

"Not them. There's a guy after me. He's going to break me in half."

He was dressed well enough that he didn't look homeless, she decided, and he didn't have the telltale tang of someone who hadn't bathed in a while. His black hair was neatly buzzed on the sides with a bit of a pomp on top.

"All right," she said finally.

"Hurry," he hissed, still looking out at the darkness.

Celeste put the car in gear and pulled into the stream of vehicles headed down the hill, braking in the sluggish traffic. The guy took a deep breath, keeping an eye on the side mirror. Once they were around the first bend he seemed to relax a little.

"What's your name?" she said.

"Rolán."

"I'm Celeste." She used the Spanish pronunciation, "ce-les-*tay*," and the clipped vowels of a native speaker, even though she didn't actually speak the language.

"Are you commuting home?"

"I had errands in the Valley. Apparently this is the wrong time of day to be coming back to the city, judging by the traffic."

"My parents live in Van Nuys. Most people out there consider the Valley to be part of Los Angeles."

She waved a hand. "You know what I mean."

"Where do you live?"

"Boyle Heights."

"It makes sense that you don't speak Spanish. Those are the original Latinos. Your family has probably been here forever."

"That doesn't mean I'm oblivious to *la raza*. I still have family connections in Zacatecas and Durango."

"Even though you can't talk to them."

She shot him a look. "I'm doing you a favor here. You don't need to be criticizing my language skills."

"I'm really just criticizing your lack of language skills."

"You're kind of a dick, you know that?"

Rolán laughed at that.

Inching ahead a few yards in the long string of brake lights, Celeste looked over at his dimly lit profile.

"So who was after you?"

"A guy named Davo. He chased me out of his yard. I can't believe he ran after me down the street.

He's no kid, and he's not really in great shape."

"You're obviously faster than he is. Who's Davo?"

"My boss," Rolán said. "Although not anymore. He has a house up there. A few blocks from where you picked me up."

"Why was he after you?"

He sighed. "Well, he has something that belongs to me. I'm trying to get it back."

"It's important enough that you were going to steal it?"

"Davo's using it to blackmail me."

Celeste eyed him sidelong. "A guy who can afford a house on Mulholland is extorting money from you."

"Not money," he said. "Labor."

"You know, I have a friend who does detective work. Maybe you could talk to him."

"He's a PI?"

"Not licensed or anything. His name is Truman. He might have some ideas about how to handle it."

Rolán folded his arms. "I can handle it myself."

"See, I have to question that. You were running down the street, and jumped into a strange woman's car."

"You don't seem all that strange."

She glared at him, and he laughed again. He

had great teeth, smooth and even, she saw.

"Maybe your friend could help me out," Rolán said. "Give me his number."

"How about I call him?"

With her thumb, she tapped on her phone, mounted on the vents next to the radio, keeping one eye on the road.

"Hey, foxy lady," Truman said when he picked up.

"I've got you on speaker," Celeste said. "I'm with a potential client."

Truman's voice dropped an octave. "Oh—hey. Greetings to you both."

"Can we swing by?"

"I'm at my place."

"It'll be forty minutes or so," she said. "There's traffic."

After she ended the call, Rolán said, "That guy sounds totally gay."

"He is totally gay."

"What I need is muscle. Someone to help me push back."

"You're making the assumption that Truman couldn't do that because he's gay."

Despite her protest, Celeste knew it was actually a valid assumption—Truman was no brawler, and he never packed a weapon.

"Can he bring the backup?" Rolán said.

"He's not that kind of detective. Just talk to

him. There might be another way to retrieve your stuff. Using brain power rather than muscle."

———•———

IN FRONT OF TRUMAN'S place, Celeste pulled up to the curb and killed the engine. Rolán gestured to the alley that ran beside the redbrick building, where a dozen tents were visible, stretching back into the darkness.

"Your friend lives on Skid Row?"

"This is technically the Fashion District," she said, grabbing her bag from the backseat. "But with seventy thousand people sleeping rough in this town, Skid Row has started to sprawl beyond its official boundaries."

Celeste got out and walked to Truman's front door, climbing the few concrete steps and pressing the button labeled BOUDREAUX.

"Girl, you've got curves," Rolán said, looking up at her, a louche grin on his face.

She frowned. "You're very observant." She knew the skirt she was wearing flattered her figure.

"I'm not, though. I didn't even notice in the car. I should have been macking on you more."

"I'm really glad you didn't."

The lock buzzed, and she pulled the door open, then led the way up the stairs to Truman's loft. Once they were inside, Celeste introduced them. Truman ran a hand through his thick dark hair and flashed a nervous smile. He'd been lounging in his boxer shorts, but to prep for his visitors he'd donned a pair of tan chinos and a green T-shirt.

"This is a huge loft," Rolán said, stepping farther into the space and taking it in. "The open ceiling is amazing."

"It used to be a warehouse. Celeste's dad helped me build the bathroom walls."

Rolán looked over the incongruous white cube. "You only built them halfway up because that's the length of a two-by-four and a sheet of drywall."

"That was Ernesto's reasoning too," Truman said. "It looks strange, but it would look stranger if the walls went all the way up."

Stepping over to the bathroom, Rolán looked inside and flicked on the light. "You could put a ceiling on it. That would make it quieter. Then you could use the space above it as storage."

"I don't really need storage space."

"If it was a warehouse, where's the loading dock and the freight elevator?"

"In the other units. The building was subdivided. This is only half of this floor."

Rolán stepped out and gestured at Truman's bed. "Is it awkward having client meetings in your bedroom?"

"It's also my kitchen and my living room and my office. I don't usually have meetings here." Truman waved his arm at the trio of sofas arranged in a square near the door. "Why don't you two sit. Do you want a soda or something?"

"Hit me," Celeste said, and went to the most comfortable of the three, the purple one against the wall.

Rolán sat adjacent to her, and Truman handed them each a bottle of Italian soda. Rolán double-clicked his tongue in thanks, and Truman sat facing Rolán on the third sofa, and set his own bottle on the coffee table.

"So where did you two meet?"

"Rolán asked me for a ride at the top of Crescent Heights. He was fleeing his former boss's house." She raised her eyebrows. "There was talk of blackmail."

Truman eyed Rolán. "What's going on?"

"This guy has something that belongs to me," Rolán said, gesturing with his bottle. "His name is Davo. I need to get it back."

"Tell me about Davo."

"He runs an import company, and he has a house up there on Mulholland. I worked for him in his warehouse, unloading containers, moving stuff into storage, loading it onto trucks."

"What kind of imports?" Truman said.

"Wooden furniture and *chvotchkays* from

Southeast Asia. Mostly from Indonesia. He resells it to shops and designers."

"What are *chvotchkays*?" Celeste said.

"It's a word Davo uses for sculptures and statues. Stuff to decorate your house that you'd put on a shelf or hang on the wall." Rolán looked around the room. "You don't really have any. It's probably an Armenian word. Davo is Armenian."

"I bet it's the same word as tchotchke," Celeste said.

"What does that mean?"

"Just what you said: decorative objects that aren't art."

"Some of them are pretty artistic."

Celeste gestured with her bottle. "If they're mass-produced in Southeast Asia, by definition they're not art."

"Celeste runs a gallery," Truman said. "Did she not tell you that?"

"I work in a gallery," Celeste said.

Rolán tipped his bottle toward her. "Got it— *chvotchkays* are not art."

"What is it that Davo has of yours that you want to get back?" Truman said.

"I'm not going to tell you that. The details don't matter. What I need is backup. I want to go up there and get it. He has a wife, but they eat out a lot. The staff only come during the day. We can go in when they're not home. Maybe tomorrow night. I know when they're not around because they park their cars in the yard. There's no garage."

Truman shook his head. "I'm not going to help you do a break-in. I can't help you at all unless I know the details."

Rolán sat back and folded his arms. "I knew this would be a waste of time."

"Maybe there's another way to get your stuff back. I can brainstorm it, go through the possibilities. It's kind of what I do."

"It's always useful to have someone else's insight," Celeste said. "Truman doesn't know you, or Davo. He can be objective."

"What's it going to cost me?"

"If I take the job, five hundred a day."

He nodded, and looked at the dark windows for a moment. Truman could see the wheels turning. Eventually Rolán spoke.

"Here's the deal. I loaned Davo my spare motorcycle helmet. He got into a hit-and-run on his own bike and killed a guy. The victim's blood is on the outside of the helmet, and my DNA is on the inside. Davo says he'll give it to the cops and frame me for it if I don't do what he says."

"If Davo was wearing it," Truman said, reaching for his soda bottle, "wouldn't his DNA be on the inside of it too?"

"I loaned it to him as a spare for his wife, but she hadn't worn it yet when he hit the guy. It was strapped to the side of his bike. So it's just my sweat on it and some dead guy's blood."

"When did this happen?"

"I don't know what day. A few weeks ago."

"Did he say where?"

"In Westmont." Rolán gestured impatiently. "The details don't matter. Davo said he hit the guy, and he didn't stop, and later he heard that he'd died."

"That's a rough neighborhood," Truman said. "They call it Murdertown. What was he doing down there?"

"He said he got off the freeway to avoid traffic."

"What's the blackmail part?" Celeste said. "What is he making you do?"

"Work for him for free." Rolán gestured helplessly. "It's not right."

"How do you know the helmet is at his house?" Truman said.

"It has to be either there or at the warehouse. It's safer to stash it at his house. At work there's always stuff moving around, and people going in and out. There's really nowhere to lock it up."

Truman watched him for a moment before he spoke. "Maybe I could talk to him for you. Try to get him to see reason."

"Don't you think I've tried talking?" Rolán scoffed. "The guy is nuts. The easiest way is just to take it from him when he's not there."

"I'm not going to help you break into his house."

"So then we have nothing to talk about."

"If you get caught, you'll do serious jail time, regardless of the hit-and-run," Truman said. "Why not give me a day or two to do some research on this guy? Maybe I can figure out how to approach it."

"How about this: if you can help me get what I want, I'll pay you. If you don't, I'm not going to pay you anything."

Truman waved his arm. "I can't work for free. How about I don't make you pay me up front, but you agree to pay me for a minimum of two days' work."

"Sure," Rolán said, his gaze even. "Let's see what you come up with."

Celeste eyed Truman and pushed her long hair back. She held two fingers to lips, as if holding an invisible cigarette, then pulled them away, and pursed her lips, and mimed blowing in the air. Her meaning was clear—she thought the guy was blowing smoke about paying him.

Rolán got up and extended his hand. Truman rose too and shook it, trying to emulate his firm grip, even though he hated the gesture.

"Let me get my computer," Truman said, and stepped toward the kitchen counter, where he washed his hands in the sink. No way did he need this guy's microbiome all over him, colonizing his skin.

Once he'd grabbed his laptop from his desk, he sat with them again.

"So what's Davo's company name?" Truman said. "And where's his business, and his house?"

"The company is just his last name—Avakian." Rolán spelled it. "The warehouse is in Vernon. I'm sure you can look up the street address."

Truman made notes, and asked some more questions, and copied down Rolán's phone number. Finally Rolán sat forward.

"I need to go back up to Mulholland tonight," he said. "To get my bike."

"I can't take you," Celeste said, setting her bottle on the coffee table. "I've got stuff to do."

"Maybe Truman could drive me up there," Rolán said, eyeing him. "As part of your detective duties."

"I don't actually have a car."

"Seriously?" Rolán frowned. "My friend works near here. Maybe if he's around he can give me a ride." He pulled out his phone and thumb-typed for a moment. Looking to Celeste, he added, "I need to get your number."

"Why is that? I'm not working for you."

"You saved my life tonight. For some reason the universe put us together. I can't just ignore that."

Celeste chuckled. "That might be a bit hyperbolic. All I did was give you a ride."

"I'm not going to pretend I know what that word means." He held her gaze. "But tonight, you believed in me. That has to mean something."

"You really do know how to spin the sweet talk," she said, and recited her phone number.

Rolán punched it into his phone, then gazed at the screen. "Luis says I can use his wheels, but he's working late." He eyed Truman. "Can you drive at all? You could bring the car back."

Truman nodded. "I can do that."

"He works at a hardware store in Westlake," he said, and stood up.

"That's not really walkable."

"It's not that far by car," Celeste said. "I can drop you there."

Truman locked his door behind them, and they walked down to the street and Celeste's little blue car. Without even asking, Rolán sat in the front, so Truman climbed in the back.

Celeste flicked on her headlights, and nosed into the street, and a few minutes later rolled into the sprawling parking lot of the big-box hardware store. She stopped near the front doors.

"Call me later," she said, eyeing Truman.

He knew she didn't have serious plans for the evening, but she also didn't want to spend it chauffeuring this guy around.

"Mwah," Truman said, and climbed out.

He followed Rolán through the doors into the brightly lit shop.

"What's your friend's name?"

"Luis," Rolán said. "Let me do the talking."

TWO

THEY FOUND LUIS IN the plumbing aisle, perched a few steps up a rolling ladder, digging through boxes on a high shelf. He was wearing the store's apron uniform, and Truman could see that he filled out his jeans nicely.

"Yo, fuckwad," Rolán called as they walked up.

"You really should be nicer to me when you're asking for favors," Luis said, and climbed down.

He had thick Latin hair cut in a natty style, and Truman saw that he'd Sharpied LUIS on his apron in big block letters, and had added an artistic 3-D effect.

"This is Truman," Rolán said. "He's going to drive your car back."

"Where did you leave your bike?"

"Up on Mulholland."

"At Davo's place." Luis gave Truman the once-over. "Do you have a driver's license?"

"I do, and no moving violations."

"My car has an automatic transmission, but if you stop at a light on a slope, it'll roll backward. You always have to use the brakes."

Truman nodded. "Got it."

Luis handed Rolán his keys, and Truman followed him out to the parking lot. They walked up on an unusual old car, a maroon hatchback with a creamy white panel that ran along the side and onto the roof.

"This is it." Rolán stepped around to the driver's door.

"It's an antique."

"People who drive these use the term 'classic.'"

"What kind of car is it?" Truman pulled the door open and got in, looking over the dash and the backseat.

"It's called a Pacer."

"There's so much glass."

"Cool, right? It's from the late seventies."

"It feels like we're sitting in a bubble."

Rolán started the engine and pulled onto the street.

"So tell me about Luis," Truman said.

"You got the vibe off him, huh. It's true—he's one of your people."

"Good to know."

"I don't think you're his type, though. He goes for Latin guys."

Rolán turned onto the freeway ramp and accelerated, nosing his way over to the left lane. He drove fast, and changed lanes whenever it gave him a speed advantage, pushing the old car hard.

"This thing really moves," Truman said, raising his voice over the road noise, "considering it's older than either one of us."

"It's about knowing how to massage the speed out of it." Rolán eyed him sidelong. "How did you get into this work, anyway? You seem kind of soft to be a detective."

"You don't get to judge me," Truman snapped. "I'm helping you out here."

"Dude—chill. I'm just saying."

"What's your definition of the opposite of soft?" he demanded. "A gangbanger? Is that your metric for what a detective is supposed to look like? If we're labeling people, that's exactly what you look like."

"I'm not a gangbanger."

"Chill out. I'm just saying."

Rolán chuckled at that. When the highway started to climb the hills, he whipped across the travel lanes and exited onto an access road.

"You change lanes fast," Truman said, "and cut across the whole highway, but you also signal each time. Why bother?"

"When you're on a motorcycle, the most dangerous thing on the road is a vehicle that doesn't signal its moves."

There it was, Truman thought. Rolán knew that specific danger from personal experience. Self-interest was the only reason he was doing it.

From the access road he turned onto a dark hillside street that climbed a hill and then crossed over the freeway. This must be Mulholland Drive, Truman realized. It was wider than most hillside streets, but still poorly lit as it wound along the ridge.

Still moving fast, Rolán navigated the curves, and eventually paused at the stoplight at Laurel Canyon. Not far past the intersection, he pulled onto a side street and slowed the car.

"That's Davo's place."

The gate stood open, and the house beyond loomed in the shadows.

"Check out the vehicles," Rolán said. "Both of them were gone when I was here before. The gold Lexus is his wife's, and Davo's car is the Bimmer."

"There's lots of those around."

"His is different. See how big it is? It's a model that's technically illegal in California, because of the emissions. You actually never see it around here. Plus it's green. Not many are that color."

"It looks black to me."

"That's because of the low light. Trust me, it's dark green."

He rolled past the house, and around a bend in the road, then pulled into a driveway and backed out again, facing the way they'd come, and stopped the car.

"There's my bike," Rolán said.

A sleek motorcycle was parked off the edge of the pavement. In the darkness it was almost invisible against the shrubbery.

"Do you want me to wait to make sure it'll start?"

He scoffed. "It'll start."

Rolán left the engine running and they both climbed out. Truman walked around to the driver's side, and adjusted the seat and the mirrors, and despite Rolán's dismissal, waited for him anyway. He watched as Rolán pulled on his helmet, shiny black with a dark visor, then started the bike and flicked on the headlight. He rolled it onto the pavement and sped up, in moments reaching the first curve and disappearing from view.

As Truman followed, gradually getting used to the feel of the old car, he caught a last glimpse of Rolán's taillight. The machinery felt loose, like adjusting the angle of the front wheels took more manipulation of the steering wheel than in a newer car. The engine seemed to rev lower too, but it sounded healthy, and overall everything about it felt laid-back.

When he pulled into the parking lot at the hardware store, he parked the Pacer where they'd found it, then walked inside and found Luis. He was with a customer, and Truman waited nearby, watching him talk earnestly about the peculiarities of furnace air filters. Such a hot guy. He had none of the edginess or the bluster that Rolán had.

The customer walked away, an air filter in hand, and Luis approached Truman.

"Is my car still in one piece?"

"It's fine, although it has a little shimmy when you get it up over about one-forty."

"Funny." Luis cracked a smile. "That car has never moved that fast, even when it was brand-new."

"You're very trusting, letting a perfect stranger drive it."

"I figured Rolán checked you out."

"It's a great car. I don't think I've ever seen one."

"There's a few of them around. The hard part is that it's expensive to maintain."

"So—do you, uh, drink, or eat food?" Truman could feel his face heating up.

Luis chuckled. "It sounds like you're trying to ask me out."

"I'm obviously not very good at it."

"Funny you should ask, though. I do in fact eat food and drink liquids. Maybe we can do something like that together."

Truman pulled out his phone, a smile spreading on his face. "Can I get your number?"

———◆———

WALKING TO THE METRO, just a couple of blocks away, Truman called Celeste.

"Drinks?" he said when she picked up. "How about that place on Spring Street?"

He rode the train a couple of stops into downtown, and climbed up out of the ground, and walked to the bar. It was an old place, but not a dive bar, with a black-and-white tile floor and the tables and chairs in dark wood. Big windows looked out onto the street.

The place wasn't crowded, and Truman sat at the bar and ordered a margarita and a gin and tonic. Not long after the bartender set down the drinks, Celeste walked in. She was still wearing what she'd had on earlier, a white blouse that showed some cleavage and a gray skirt, but she had her evening makeup on. They exchanged an air kiss before she climbed on the next stool.

"Thanks for digging up a client," he said, clinking his margarita glass against her highball.

"I wonder if that was a mistake. It doesn't seem like he's a good fit for you."

Truman wiped the margarita salt off his lip. "Because what he really wants is someone to bully his boss?"

"That, and the fact that Rolán agreed so quickly to your payment proposal." She pushed her hair behind her ear. "It means he's going to stiff you."

"I'm thinking maybe I can get what he wants and make him pay me before I hand it over."

"That sounds like extortion," Celeste said, and tipped her glass toward him before she took a sip.

"I have to try. I was thinking about it—does his story feel a little off? Hit-and-run and a frame-up? Who would do that? If I were Davo, I would have washed off the helmet to get rid of the evidence."

"Rolán is your client. Don't you have to go with what he tells you?"

"I'm working for him, but I don't have to believe everything he says."

On Celeste's other side, a guy in a security guard's uniform walked up to the bar to talk to the bartender. Truman sat up and leaned back to get a look at his butt.

Celeste glanced at the guy, then turned back. "What is your deal with cops?"

"He's not a cop."

"Is it the uniform, or the sidearm?"

"I'm just admiring the view."

She waved a hand. "Should we get another round? I took the metro so I could drink."

Celeste leaned forward to summon the bartender, not hesitating to show a bit of cleavage to get his attention. She ordered another round, then paid the guy when he set down the glasses. The place was getting more crowded and louder, and as they drank they chatted and enjoyed the vibe.

Eventually Celeste said, "Enough?"

Truman nodded and drained his tumbler as he got up, and they went out to the street. Celeste looped her arm through his as they walked the few blocks to the metro station, and once she was headed down the stairs, Truman turned south toward home, skirting the edge of Skid Row. The night air was starting to cool off as fall got closer, but it was still warm enough for shirtsleeves.

Once he got upstairs, he peeled off his clothes, and killed the lights, and climbed into bed with the book he'd found back when he'd started in this business, Biff Sturgis's *Eleven Steps to Becoming a Hard-Nosed Detective*. It had been written in the 1930s, and covered topics like packing a heater, throwing a sucker punch, and how to wear brass knuckles, none of which Truman ever planned to do, but other ideas it contained were still relevant, and it had helped him a lot. Originally he'd found it in the public library, but it was so useful that he'd bought his own copy from an online used-book dealer.

Savoring the smell of the antique paper, he flipped to the index to find the section on negotiating with clients. Biff's advice was pointed:

> Get the cash up front, and get a signed contract. If the client doesn't pay the balance owed, threatening to sue for breach of contract can give you some leverage. Don't bother to sue anybody—only the lawyers make money on lawsuits. The best way to avoid the problem is to get paid up front.
>
> Set your rates before you have the deliverables in hand, whether it's tangibles or just information. Otherwise the client might feel extorted. A man who feels pinched might just pull his rod and give you permanent lead poisoning. A woman in that position might just take out your eye with her hatpin.

Celeste had said the same thing—Rolán was never going to pay him, not unless he had the motorcycle helmet to barter with. He'd blown it. Biff would be very disappointed.

THREE

THE HOUSE WAS QUIET when Celeste woke up, as both her parents left early for their jobs. She loved this time of day, when she got ready for work, luxuriating in the pleasure of having the place to herself.

Before she got dressed, she opened her jewelry box and lifted out the tray, scrabbling around in the bottom for a Ritalin tab. Just a half. Just enough to brighten things up, sharpen the edges on the day. She bit it in two, and ground it between her teeth, and dropped the other half back into the box.

Dark trousers and a fitted jacket, she decided, and then did her eyes in the mirror. In the kitchen she made coffee and toast, and was sitting at the kitchen table smearing it with marmalade when the side door swung open and Ernesto stepped in. Dressed for work, in jeans and a plaid shirt, he was barrel-chested, with graying hair, and his belly protruded a little over his belt.

"What are you doing here?" Celeste demanded.

He laughed and stood in the kitchen doorway. "It's my house, *mija*."

"Morning is my quiet time. When I can enjoy the place without you and that wife of yours hogging up the bathroom."

"Forgive the interruption, your highness. I'll be leaving again in a minute. Are you working today?"

"That's the plan."

"If you're home this evening, maybe we can give your mother a break and walk down to those street-food vendors."

She gestured with her half-eaten toast. "I'd love that."

———

WHEN TRUMAN GOT UP, he brewed some espresso with his slick new machine, one of the few upgrades he'd made with the windfall he and Celeste had acquired on his first job as a detective. At his desk under the big multipane windows, set high in the wall to illuminate the erstwhile warehouse rather than to provide a view, he sipped at the little cup and searched for details on Davo's company.

Avakian Imports had a utilitarian website that displayed some of the products it handled. It seemed to be mostly furniture made of rattan and dark-stained tropical wood. The photos made the stuff look nice enough, but he knew rattan was light, and it was never very durable.

The tchotchkes included wooden statues of birds and deer, and those pairs of stone lions that stood guard in front of temples, and woven rattan vases shaped like bottles and decanters. That seemed less than useless, as you could never put water in them.

There were other mentions of Davo on a couple of sites that talked about furniture, and something about an Armenian church that mentioned his name in passing, but nothing in the search results made Davo look shady. When people had been sued or embroiled in criminal court cases, their names popped up, but Davo wasn't cited in that realm.

A woman with the same surname came up in the results, on a business-to-business page that listed her as an interior decorator. Truman clicked through to find a flashy website with terse breezy copy: "Working from her home in the Hollywood Hills, Mariam brings glamour to interior spaces and joy to the hearts of her clients." The images of styled rooms showed more clutter than glamour, but maybe that was subjective.

This might be Davo's wife—the one who drove the gold Lexus. Grabbing his phone, he dialed Rolán, glad that he picked up.

"Is Davo's wife named Mariam?"Truman said.

"That sounds right."

"Does she run a decorating business?"

"That's her," Rolán said. "She gets furniture from the warehouse sometimes. Big hair, lots of jewelry, fancy dresser. They type you'd call 'ma'am.'"

"I think I'll talk to her. It might get me closer to your helmet."

"How would that happen?"

"It looks like she works from home. Maybe I can get invited into the house."

"That might work, but I'm the one who needs to get into that house."

"This way, nobody's committing a felony," Truman said. "Let me see if I can look the place over. I'll check for an office or a storeroom."

"That could be useful, but you don't really know what you're looking for."

"It's a motorcycle helmet, right? That's pretty hard to hide. What color is it?"

Rolán huffed. "Black."

"The other thing is, you have to start paying me."

"Sure, I can pay you. Not today, though. Let me know what you find out."

———◆———

THE GALLERY WHERE CELESTE worked was in the Arts District downtown. She pulled into the alley and parked near the back door, in one of the spots demarcated by thin yellow lines on the asphalt. The other space was already occupied by the familiar obnoxious luxury SUV that belonged to the gallery owner, Saffron.

Twisting her key to open the back door, Celeste stepped inside. The alarm was already turned off, and she walked into the big space. A century ago it had been a factory, and now it was mostly one big open room, with concrete floors and plain white walls. The factory windows just below the ceiling provided excellent lighting for visual art.

There were two small rooms on the mezzanine, where the foreman and the bookkeepers once worked, now serving as offices for her and Saffron. Pausing at the foot of the blue-painted metal staircase, Celeste called up, "I'm here."

Saffron called back with a perfunctory greeting but didn't appear. The door to the street was already unlocked, Celeste saw, and the sign in the window had been turned over to tell the world it was OPEN.

Sometimes she wondered why they bothered—there was next to no foot traffic, even on weekends. The gallery's business was high-end artworks, which meant it had fewer customers who spent more, and the place wasn't reliant on walk-ins. Most of the time it was like this, empty and quiet.

A glass-topped desk sat near the front entrance, and Celeste settled in, setting her bag on the floor beneath it. The current exhibition, "Dark Depths of the Surrealist Soul," was one she'd curated with Saffron. They'd found three local surrealist painters who all worked in dark colors, and the pieces gave the gallery a heavy feeling, even though surrealism was inherently light. From talking to the artists, they hadn't been able to pin down whether it was just a fleeting coincidence that different people were creating similar things, influenced by the zeitgeist, or whether it was an emerging movement.

In any case the show had been successful, as they'd already sold several pieces. Celeste was happy to get the commission for working with the clients, even though most of them were Saffron's moneyed friends and connections.

She and Saffron had cooked up a plan to write for an art journal about dark surrealism as a noteworthy new trend, partly because it might be true and partly to get attention for the show.

Celeste would have to do the writing, and she needed to get on it today. Looking around the gallery, the heaviness of the paintings made the place feel even more somber than usual. At least there would be few interruptions as she settled into a day of research and writing.

———•———

TRUMAN DIALED THE PHONE number listed for Mariam Avakian's interior decorating business, surprised that she picked up on the first ring.

"Brilliance by Mariam," she said.

"Is that the name of your company?"

"It's new—I'm trying it out. What do you think?"

"I love it," Truman said. "I actually need some brilliance in my life."

"I'm so glad you called," she said, her voice rising in pitch. Truman had to pull the phone away from his ear. "What kind of help do you need?"

"I have a loft downtown that's pretty bare. I only have a few pieces of furniture. I think it needs design work."

"This sounds urgent," Mariam said. "If you're available, I can come by today."

"I can be home," Truman said, and recited his address.

"Is that in the Arts District?"

"The Fashion District. My block is close to Skid Row, so it feels a little rough, and you'll see the homeless camps. But it's safe to park on the street in the daytime."

After he'd ended the call, Truman dialed Celeste.

"I'm working," she said when she picked up.

"I bet there's a huge crowd in there on Friday morning."

"My career involves much more than managing the looky-loos."

"So it turns out Davo's wife is an interior decorator," Truman said. "She's coming over to my place this afternoon."

"My god—why?"

"It might give me a way to get into their house. I think that's where her office is. Do you want to meet her?"

"I don't know. I've got some stuff to do."

"Saffron doesn't care if you're there or not. This woman sounds like a lot of fun—her business is called Brilliance by Mariam. Her website is plastered with leopard, cheetah, and zebra prints. If I didn't know she was a woman, I'd assume she was a drag queen."

"You should have led with that," Celeste said. "I love her already. What time will she be there?"

———·———

A WHILE LATER, CONTENT that she had a solid start on her article, appropriately blowing the lid off a burgeoning breakthrough in surrealism, Celeste called up the stairs: "I'm going out for a while."

Saffron came out of her office and stood on the walkway, leaning on the railing. Her black hair was piled on her head, and she was wearing a casual blue sweater rather than something dressy. That meant she had no meetings today.

"You can leave the door open," Saffron said. "I'm here for a while."

"I'll be back in a couple hours."

"We've got a whale coming in on Sunday afternoon."

"Nice. I'm on the schedule to be here. Do you want me to handle it?"

"I think that would be best," Saffron said. "I have brunch plans."

"How big a whale?"

"Smallish. She has a dental practice. She's in the market for one piece."

"Dentists are technical people," Celeste said. "I know which pieces to push. Send me the details."

"Ciao, darling," she said, and waggled her fingers.

Truman's building was just a few minutes' drive, and Celeste pulled up out front, waiting behind a delivery van while the driver trotted back from the shops across the street. Once he'd jumped behind the wheel, and killed his flashers, and pulled into the traffic, she maneuvered her car next to the parking meter.

Truman buzzed her in, and when she got up the stairs and stepped into his loft, she found him standing by the kitchen counter, wearing a blue collared shirt and dress pants.

"Wow," Celeste said. "You tidied."

"I just hung up my clothes and put the laundry away."

"You made your bed. This may be the first time I've ever seen that."

Truman scoffed. "Do you want a soda?"

"I'm OK. What's your story going to be?"

"It's simple. My place needs decorating."

"How are you going to explain my presence?"

Before he could answer, the door buzzer sounded, and he stepped over to the box.

"Come on up," Truman shouted, pressing the mike button, not sure if he'd be heard through the static.

He pulled open the door, and a moment later Mariam appeared. Coiffed to substantial volume, her dark hair had patchy blond highlights. She wore a leopard-print blouse under a long fuchsia-colored overcoat, and jewelry dangled from her ears, on her fingers, around her neck. Almost instantly he was struck by a shock wave of flowery perfume.

"You must be Truman," she said, and beamed, and clasped both his hands in hers.

Why did people do things like that? Now he had to act like both his hands were dead until he had a chance to rinse them off.

He returned her smile. "A pleasure. This is Celeste."

"You're very pretty." Mariam grasped Celeste's hands. "You have such a spacious home."

"Oh—I don't live here," Celeste said.

Mariam nodded sagely. "I can see it needs a woman's touch."

"It definitely needs something."

"You make a lovely couple," Mariam said, stepping back and looking them over. "Are you moving in after you get married?"

Truman gestured vaguely. "Uh ..."

"That's right," Celeste said. "At the moment it's Truman's loft, but as you can see, it has plenty of space for two."

Truman frowned at her, but Mariam didn't notice, instead clapping her hands and beaming.

"I love weddings. Have you set a date?"

"Not yet," Celeste said. "We're thinking springtime."

Mariam walked farther into the space, past the white cube of the bathroom, and then the bed and the clothes rack, looking things over. After a full circuit she came back to where they were standing.

"You didn't tell me you had a fiancée," she said.

Truman folded his arms. "I wasn't sure she'd be here today. I thought she had to work."

"She has to be here," Mariam said. "It's her house too."

"That's right, bub," Celeste said, shooting him a look. "It's my house too."

"What kind of work do you do?" Mariam said, eyeing Truman.

"Mostly research."

"That's exciting. Science is so interesting." She turned to Celeste. "And what field are you in?"

"I work in an art gallery."

Mariam's eyebrows shot up. "Then you don't need me to decorate your house. You must already know what's elegant."

"I think it's a different skill set. I deal with visual art, not big three-dimensional spaces," Celeste said, and waved an arm at the room.

Mariam touched her fingertips to her temples, revealing her blood-red manicure. "Oh, my god," she shrieked. "Brainwave."

"What's wrong?" Truman said, his brow furrowing as he stepped closer.

"Celeste could source wall art for my decorating clients."

Truman took a breath. "I thought you were having an aneurism."

Mariam stepped closer to Celeste, and flipped back her fuchsia coattails, and put her hands on her hips. "Some people just want movie posters or Cézanne prints, but some have more money. They can afford better taste."

"I would love to help you with that," Celeste said.

"What kind of gallery are you with?"

"It's near here, in the Arts District. Most of my clients are investors. They don't care so much about the content of an artwork, but they want works that will sell for more in ten years."

"So it's expensive."

"Not exclusively, but it does tend to be high-end."

"What about people who just want pretty things?"

Celeste nodded. "I can find that kind of artist too."

"We should definitely do some work together."

Watching them, Truman had to grin. They were making a connection.

"What about this place, Mariam?" Celeste said. "What's your vision?"

Mariam gestured upward. "Well, the open ceiling is beautiful, so I wouldn't want to hide that. Looking at this floor, however, makes me sad. The concrete has centuries of damage."

"Doesn't that give it character?" Truman said.

Mariam's eyes narrowed. "Using that defini-tion, the landfill is the most characterful place in town."

"So what's your idea for the floor?" Celeste said.

"I'm thinking marble."

Truman folded his arms. "What color marble?"

"White," she said, her tone hushed. "White and polished to a high gloss."

"It sounds like I'd have to mop it."

"Beautiful things require sacrifice, Truman." She held his gaze. "What's the square footage here? About eighteen hundred?"

"Twenty-two fifty."

"That's going to require a significant amount of stone. We'll be able to get a decent price on it." She stepped over to the windows and spread her arms in the air. "Here I see curtains, from the rafters to the floor."

"That's fifteen feet," Truman said.

"We can do it. I can get rails with remote-controlled motors to open and close them. I'm thinking silver lamé fabric, or maybe silver chain mail." She turned to face them. "It's not actual chain mail. It's made of plastic, so it's light, and it won't pull the rafters down. It just looks like metal."

Truman nodded. "That sounds beautiful."

Mariam stepped toward the bathroom. "The boxy shape is pleasing to the eye, but it's awfully white. I'm thinking we'll paint it either vermilion or Santorini blue. We'll pin that down once we settle on the rest."

"Vermilion is red?" Truman said.

"It's the red of imperial China." Walking toward his bed, a queen mattress on a metal frame that he'd found at a thrift store, Mariam waved her arms.

"Because you're newlyweds, the bed should be on a platform. We have the space to do it. I'm thinking three steps up, and an organdy canopy all around. That will create a room within the room. A bedroom in the midst of the space."

"What colors?" Celeste said.

"Orange, to match the brickwork, perhaps?"

"You can never have too much organdy," Truman said.

Mariam touched his arm. "My sentiments exactly." As she stepped over to the kitchen sink and cabinets, she spread her arms wide. "We can hide the kitchen area with simple white curtains. I think we'd make them the same height as the bathroom walls. We can run a rail across to this pillar."

"So you're thinking a lot of curtains," Celeste said.

"To break up the space. You'll need to pick the fabrics. I couldn't bring my sample books with me because there are so many genres. I had to know what we're dealing with first."

"If it's easier," Truman said quickly, "we could come by your office to look at them."

"I actually work from home."

"What neighborhood are you in?" Celeste said.

"The Hollywood Hills. Near Crescent Heights and Mulholland."

"I know where that is," she said. "It's easy enough to stop by."

"Why not?" Mariam flashed a smile. "When are you both free?"

"In the morning?" Celeste said, and eyed Truman.

"Fine with me." He eyed Mariam. "You don't mind working on Saturday?"

"Oh, sweetheart, I work when the work finds me."

"I hear you," he said, and pulled out his phone as Mariam rattled off her address. Even though he knew where it was, Truman thumb-typed it into his contact list.

"I'm very excited to work with you," Mariam said, and stepped toward the door. With a final good-bye and a swirl of fuchsia, she was gone.

"I'll take that soda now," Celeste said, once

Truman had closed the door.

"Blood orange or pomegranate?"

"Whichever one will be gentler on my visual receptors." She sank onto one of the sofas. "That coat."

"Amazing, right?" Truman stepped over from the fridge and handed her a bottle, then sat down. "What's organdy?"

"You talked about it like you knew."

"That kitchen curtain idea would make it look like a hospital in here."

"And marble floors would make it look like a mortuary."

"I can't believe you're going to work with her on sourcing art," Truman said, gesturing with his bottle. "Biff Sturgis says 'Play your cards close to the vest.' It means don't tell people too much about what you're doing."

Celeste frowned. "It's nothing to do with your case. I won't blow your cover. Selling her some art is a legit opportunity for me to make some money."

"Rolán says Davo is a crook. Doesn't that imply that Mariam is too?"

"You said you thought Rolán was lying to you. Maybe he's the crook."

"I did say that, didn't I." Truman took a sip of his soda. "It was a brilliant idea to pose as my fiancée."

"She kind of made that assumption, and I just went along with it. I'm amazed that she bought it."

Truman frowned. "Why would it be unlikely? We're the same age, and in similar hotness categories."

"Rolán pegged you as gay from a brief phone call," Celeste said. "Before he even met you."

"Mariam is a little older. Less tuned in. Plus rich folks get more limited exposure to reality. Money insulates them from it."

Celeste's phone buzzed, and she pulled it out to look. "Speak of the devil."

"Rolán?"

"I think so. It's an 818 number, and he's a Valley boy."

When she answered, he said, "It's Rolán. Remember me?"

"Of course. You're the guy who carjacked me yesterday."

"That's not quite how I remember it. I'd like to see you again."

"That might be fun," Celeste said, and chuckled. "There's actually a thing I want to see. It's downtown, not far from Figueroa."

"What's it going to set me back?"

"It's free." She rolled her eyes for Truman's benefit, then set up a time to meet him.

Once she'd set the phone down, Truman said,

"Your voice goes so high when you're talking to a hot guy."

She frowned. "No it doesn't."

"You're going on a date?"

"I'm taking him to see an exhibition. We'll see if he can tolerate it."

"You should talk to him about Davo. Maybe you can find out if there's more going on that he's not telling us."

"I'm sure it'll come up." Celeste rose. "I should get back to work."

Once she'd left, Truman went over to turn on the fan near the bed. Hopefully it would disperse the lingering haze of Mariam's floral perfume.

He should get his own date lined up, he realized, especially if Celeste wouldn't be around tonight for drinks. Pulling out his phone, he sat at his desk and sent Luis a text:

Want to get together this evening?

His reply came soon after:

I work until 6. I'll be hungry. Let's meet somewhere with food.

Truman wrote back with the name of a place that was between here and Luis's store. He soon responded:

I'll be there.

Truman had to smile. Just getting to this point meant half the work was done.

FOUR

CELESTE TEXTED HER PARENTS that she wouldn't be joining them for street tacos this evening, then locked up the gallery, and went out the back door to the alley and her car. The security guy was strolling by, and they exchanged a wave as she got in behind the wheel.

His job was to keep the homeless from setting up camp back here. The businesses lining the alley chipped in to pay for the service, and so far it had worked. Otherwise it would look like Truman's alley, and she and everyone else would be afraid to park back here, or even open the back door.

As she drove toward the street, past the guard, Celeste heaved a sigh. It was messed up that things had come to this point, that they needed to pay private security to keep the hordes of impoverished humans off a public roadway.

The streets were busy with Friday traffic, and she pushed it out of her mind as she drove over to the Financial District. The garages under the office towers were already charging the more reasonable flat evening rate, so she turned into one and parked near the elevator.

Up at street level again, she walked to the busy intersection at Seventh Street and scanned the pedestrians. She didn't have to wait long before Rolán appeared, in his leather biker jacket, walking toward her, a strut in his step. He actually had a decent body, she realized, watching him move.

When he spotted her, he jutted his chin and walked over, holding her gaze as he beamed beatifically. It was a valuable asset—he had to know the power of that brilliant smile. He'd probably used it his whole life to charm relatives, teachers, cops.

"You look amazing," Rolán said.

"It's how I dress for work." She grinned and ran a hand into her dark hair, pushing it back.

"So where are we going?"

"It's right up the block." She gestured, and they set off, walking abreast. "There's an exhibition in the lobby of an office building."

"If you work in an art gallery," Rolán said, sidestepping an oncoming pedestrian, "isn't this like work?"

"Yes and no. I'm also interested in art. It's what I got my degree in."

"I wonder if you're too smart for me."

"Going to school doesn't mean I'm smart," Celeste said, eyeing him. "I don't know you, but I can tell you're no dummy."

Rolán briefly put his hand in the small of her back. "You certainly know how to say the right things."

They stepped into the lobby of an office tower, and Celeste saw the sign for the exhibition, pointing the way up a set of steps that led to the mezzanine.

"Whose place is this?" Rolán said.

"It belongs to a bank. They must rent a lot of this building—their logo is on the top."

"Why does a bank have an art exhibition?" he said, following her up the stairs. He lowered his voice, as if he were out of his element, somewhere he wasn't supposed to be.

"It's like advertising. It shows the world you're doing something civic-minded for society, not just extracting wealth from it."

The security guard at the door to the little gallery space nodded to Celeste as she walked in. His eyes lingered a moment on Rolán, but Rolán ignored the guy and stepped inside. It was a small room with a dozen or so paintings displayed on the walls. Several people stood around studying them. Celeste looked at the one nearest the entrance, then stepped to the next, and the next.

"You don't need very long with each one," Rolán said.

"I know all these works," she said, scanning the room. "It's standard investment-grade art. Exactly what a banker would buy. Big names with value that will probably increase over time. Like real estate or mine leases or stocks."

"This one looks kind of familiar. Who are the artists?"

"Manet, Monet, Renoir. I'm sure they'll be a Degas and a Cézanne somewhere here. The genre is called impressionism."

"Even I've heard those names."

"They were important in the nineteenth century. I guess they're still important if you're a banker." Celeste glanced around the room. "We can go."

"Are you sure? You haven't seen them all."

"I can't really see any of them. They're all behind glass. It's a great way to protect your investment, but no one can see the brushwork. That's the only value in seeing this kind of work in person. Here they've effectively prevented it."

They stepped past the watchful guard and walked out to the street.

"Do you want to get a drink?" Celeste said.

Rolán cracked a smile. "I was hoping that was next."

———◆———

GETTING READY FOR HIS night out, Truman ran some gel into his hair, then spent a few minutes working it to make it look like he hadn't worked on it. A shirt with a collar, he decided, and the rust-red pants that flattered his butt. He didn't have the kind of body that turned heads, but these pants made the best of what he did have. He'd forgo the jacket, as lately the September evenings had been almost as warm as midsummer.

Once he'd locked up his place and trotted down the stairs, he set off at his commuter pace, the resolute stride of someone who walked a lot, rapidly skirting the edges of Skid Row, headed toward the Financial District. He was looking forward to this—his stomach was growling, and Luis was a total snack.

———◆———

AFTER A FEW BLOCKS' walk, on a crowded stretch of Seventh Street, Celeste led Rolán into a brightly lit bar. It had a low tin ceiling and bare floors that amplified the noise. The place wasn't expensive, but it had lots of white, in the tables and chairs and walls, and that made it look fresh.

"Table or barstool?" Rolán said as they stepped inside.

"We'll sit at the bar," she said firmly. "Tables are for amateurs."

Rolán laughed at that and followed her. The room was warm, and he peeled off his leather jacket and folded it on the stool next to her before he sat on it. It gave her some insight into him, Celeste realized—the garment was utilitarian, not a prized possession to be coddled and carefully hung in a secure spot.

The bartender, a woman in a black vest with her hair pulled tightly back, stepped over, and Celeste ordered a martini.

The woman raised her eyebrows. "Gin or vodka?"

"Who would put vodka in a martini?" Celeste demanded.

"We get weirdos in here sometimes. People from faraway places with messed-up customs. You know how it is."

"Gin works for me. The cheaper the better."

The woman winked at her and looked to Rolán.

"Should I do that?" Rolán said, "or should I just have a beer?"

Celeste leaned over to bump his shoulder with her own. "You should order what you want."

"Dos Equis," he said to the bartender, then

turned to Celeste. "I haven't been in here before."

"It's fairly new. Connected to the restaurant next door. Before that, this space was an Irish pub." She frowned. "Does the fact that I know all that make me sound like a barfly?"

He grinned and shook his head, then turned to survey the room. When the drinks came, Celeste pulled out a wad of cash.

"Let me pay," Rolán said.

"You said you were unemployed."

"Partly unemployed."

"Well, you can get the next round." She set some bills on the bar, and watched as the bartender whisked them away. "So what does partly unemployed mean?"

"I tried working part-time at my cousin's tire shop. It's dirty work compared to the warehouse. I don't think I'll stick with it."

"Is the tire shop out in Van Nuys?"

Rolán's eyebrows rose. "I told you I live there?"

"You told me your parents live there," Celeste said. "Davo's warehouse is in Vernon?"

"Right, but I'm not going there anymore."

"You said he was making you work for free."

He scowled. "We don't need to talk about that. Your friend Truman told me he was going to meet Davo's wife. I'm not sure how that'll help."

"If he gets into her house, he might be able to find your helmet for you."

"I want to get in there myself. Maybe Truman can explain the layout for me."

She eyed him sidelong. "You really are focused on that house."

Rolán gestured with his beer bottle. "So that exhibition didn't seem very important to you. What's the style of art today?"

Celeste sat up and sipped her drink. "What's trendy right now is called postmodernism."

"Is that the paintings of soup cans?"

"That's part of it. As a movement it means that the technique doesn't matter, only the idea in the piece. People come into the gallery, and see an artwork, and say, 'A nine-year-old could do that.' It may be true, but a nine-year-old didn't do it. The artist is the one who had the idea."

Rolán was watching her intently, a hint of a smile on his face. Celeste grinned and looked away.

"I really like talking to you," he said.

"I can't believe you're that interested in art."

"You're into it, and I'm interested in you."

Celeste lifted her glass and tapped it on his bottle. "Well, you're an excellent listener."

———·———

THE PLACE THEY WERE meeting was a brewpub, and when Truman walked in, he saw Luis was already parked at a booth, absorbed in his phone, his face illuminated by the blue glow of its screen.

He looked up as Truman slid onto the bench across from him and flashed a smile.

"I'm so glad you didn't want to go to a boy bar."

"I can't afford the competition," Truman said. "Here it's boring straight guys from the local offices."

"Plus plant-based burgers." When the server appeared, Luis pointed to the menu. "I want to try this hefeweizen."

"The same," Truman said, and they both ordered burgers.

"I like this place," Luis said, once the guy had stepped away. "I was looking at the building's facade. It's really beautiful."

"It's one of the oldest office buildings in this neighborhood," Truman said. "It went up around 1910. This street was called the Banking District. During Prohibition there was a speakeasy in the basement. You could walk all the way to city hall in the underground delivery tunnels."

"You sound like the Einstein of old buildings."

Truman laughed. "I used to be a tour guide."

"Before you started working as a detective?"

He nodded. "It sounds like Rolán told you what we're doing."

"You were driving my car," Luis said. "Of course he told me."

He paused as the server set down their beer glasses, and they clinked them together.

"What kind of tour guide were you?"

"I worked for travel companies that brought groups to town."

"Those bus tours that go past the movie stars' houses?"

"I did those," Truman said, "and walking tours in this part of town. The cemetery tours were always fun."

"How's the detective business?"

"Better paid."

"What do people hire you to do?" Luis said.

"Find stuff, or find people, or figure out whether their spouse is lying to them." Truman sipped his beer. "What have you got going on besides the hardware store?"

"I take some classes at community college. If I can save up enough, I'll go full-time next year."

"Right on," Truman said, and leaned back as their food arrived. Once he'd had a few bites, he said, "What are you studying?"

"Philosophy." He grinned. "I know that's useless in the labor market."

"You never know. So where do you live?"

Luis waved dismissively, and spoke through a mouthful of food. "With my parents."

The guy might be younger than he thought, Truman realized, watching him eat. But then

Celeste lived with her parents, and she was no kid.

When the check arrived, Truman picked it up. "Will you let me pay? Because you're a college student."

"Do you earn enough to play sugar daddy?"

"No—but it's just one meal."

Luis nodded. "Sure. Thanks."

Once they were out on the street, Truman turned to face him. "Do you want to come over to my pad?"

"You're on your own in that big place? No roommates?"

He studied Luis's face. Obviously Rolán had also told him about his loft. "I live alone."

"Is the plan to mess around?"

"Ideally," Truman said, "but I've got a bottle of vodka in the freezer if you want to do that instead."

Luis grinned. "I won't need vodka, son."

———•———

AFTER THEY'D FINISHED THE round, Celeste said, "I should go. This was fun."

"Can I see you again?" Rolán said.

"Why not?"

They walked out together, and Celeste paused on the sidewalk.

"Are you on your motorcycle?"

"I parked up that way," he said, gesturing with his chin as he pulled his jacket on.

"I'm headed back to Fig."

His brow furrowed. "Can I kiss you good night?"

"What are you waiting for?"

Rolán grinned and leaned in, grasping her arm and meeting her mouth. His was warm, and tasted of yeasty beer, but he was good at this. After a moment she pulled away, and briefly cradled his cheek.

"Good night, Rolán."

As she walked up the block, Celeste felt flushed, partly from the gin and partly from that kiss. The sidewalk felt light under her feet, and she couldn't help but smile.

———◆———

LUIS'S PACER WAS PARKED up the street, and he paused to unlock the passenger door for Truman.

"I love this car," he said, waiting for Luis to walk around and climb in. "It's so groovy."

"People either love it or hate it. Even brand-new, it was unique."

Truman directed him to his street, and Luis pulled up to a meter in front of his building. He killed the engine and looked around.

"Is it safe to park here?"

"Let me talk to one of my neighbors."

Truman climbed out and stepped over to the alley beside his building, standing at the edge of the row of tents.

"Angel," he called, and listened, and when he got no response, tried "Beretta."

A minute later the guy appeared, strolling out of the gloom. He had a shaggy brown beard, and his hair was tied back. Despite the warmth of the evening he wore a puffy winter jacket.

"What's up, Sunshine?"

"I wanted to hire you to keep an eye on my friend's car for a few hours." Truman pointed out the Pacer, where Luis was standing at the curb.

"Sure," Beretta said. "Four bits."

"How about a sawbuck?"

"That's a lower tier of service. I might have to subcontract the work."

"Fine by me," Truman said, "as long as the car is safe."

Beretta gestured expansively. "I'll put the word out."

Truman dug in his pocket and palmed the ten, and passed it to him, then motioned for Luis to join him at the door to his building.

"Do you know all the homeless folks that well?" Luis said, as they trudged up the stairs.

"Just a couple of them."

"He asked you for fifty cents, and you gave him ten bucks."

"Four bits means fifty bucks," Truman said. "At least in that alley."

Stepping into his loft, Luis stood and looked around. "Rolán was right. This place is huge, and there's nothing in it."

"There's lots of stuff in it." Truman watched him as he took it in.

"I think he meant valuable stuff." He turned to face him. "Not that I'm dissing the thrift-store look."

Truman stepped closer, and ran a hand into his hair, and leaned in to kiss him. Luis's mouth was taut, and intent, and responded in the most pleasing way. Reaching for his shirt, Luis unbuttoned it, running his hands over Truman's chest.

"You're so hot."

Leading him toward his bed, Truman pulled his shirt off, and soon they were both undressed. Truman pushed him onto the mattress and then climbed up to straddle him. Luis was already hard, and Truman ran his hands over his skin. It was warm and lean.

Luis squeezed his cock. "Can I fuck you?"

Truman leaned over to grab a condom from the drawer in the night table and ripped it open for him. Holding his gaze, Luis rolled it on himself, then shifted position, and leaned into him. He seemed confident for someone his age.

Soon Luis pushed into him, and Truman

gasped with the intensity of it. Luis built up to pounding him, and then came, and leaned in to meet Truman's mouth. He stroked his cock and brought Truman to climax.

Once he'd pulled away, Truman stretched out and spent a minute catching his breath, luxuriating in the warmth of Luis's body.

"That was fun," Luis said. "Can I stay for a while?"

"Of course."

Luis got up and walked over to the bathroom. When he came back he grabbed his jeans, in a rumpled pile on the floor, and pulled his phone from the pocket. Back in bed, he spent a moment thumb-typing.

"I have to let my mom know I'm not coming home. Otherwise she worries."

"I'm afraid to ask you how old you are," Truman said.

Luis chuckled and set his phone aside. "I'm not jail bait, if that's what you're worried about."

FIVE

AYLIGHT WAS STREAMING IN the high windows when Truman woke, and he saw that Luis was getting dressed.

"I can make coffee if you want."

"I have to go," Luis said, snatching up his shirt. "Will that homeless guy want more money for watching my car?"

"His name is Beretta. If he asks, tell him you'll get him next time."

"Does knowing his name give me power over him or something? Like Rumpelstiltskin?"

"He's a human being in this world," Truman said. "Most people like to be known by their name."

Luis stepped over and leaned in for a lingering kiss, his hand cradling Truman's head.

"Bye, Truman."

Once he was gone, Truman got out of bed, and made coffee, and got dressed. He'd eaten some breakfast and was on his second espresso when the door buzzer sounded. Stepping over to the box, he pressed the button to unlock it, not bothering to ask who it was—Celeste was due.

The deadbolt was still unlocked from when Luis had left, so he went to start an espresso for her.

When she stepped in, he said, "Coffee?"

"Hit me."

"I love that skirt," Truman said, checking out her look. It was indigo blue, with a hibiscus print, and fell just below the knee.

"I figured it fit with my cover for Mariam. Art world operator, knows her trade, soon to be married."

"You're so good at this stuff. Biff Sturgis would call you a natural."

"That's high praise from someone who lived through the Great Depression."

Truman brought the steaming demitasse cup to her, and they sat on the sofas. Celeste took a sip before she set the cup on the coffee table.

"How was your night out?" Truman said.

"Rolán is actually kind of sweet."

He frowned. "I hope you're not going to get sticky about the guy. He's my client."

"I'm not crushing on him." She waved a hand. "Besides, I saw him first."

"Did he say any more about Davo?"

She told him about their conversation, and what Rolán had said. "I think he's pretty intent on getting into Davo's house."

"That doesn't make a whole lot of sense, if his only goal is to get his helmet back."

"He thinks you're going to case the place for him. You'll tell him the layout, and then he'll go break in himself and find it."

"I should have asked Luis more about Rolán," Truman said. "I think they're close."

"That's Rolán's friend with the car?"

"I saw him last night."

"Out, or in?"

"Both."

Celeste scoffed. "You bust me for being inappropriate, and you're the one who's sleeping with your client's friends."

"On some level I guess that's not ideal."

Sitting up, she drained her cup. "Mariam is expecting us. You need a better shirt."

Truman glanced down at the comfortable polo he was wearing. "You think?"

"It doesn't have to be a date-night shirt, but wear one with a collar. Like what you had on yesterday to meet her."

He walked over to his clothes rack and found a

green dress shirt that had a bit of a sheen to it, and pulled it on, and tucked it into his chinos. Once he'd grabbed his keys and his wallet, he followed Celeste down to the street and her little blue car.

Even on Saturday the neighborhood was busy with clothing industry activity—delivery vans clogging the street, retailers with garment racks wheeled out onto the sidewalk, and the stream of pedestrians on the hunt for bargains.

"The navigation app says take the freeway," Truman said. "You can get on Mulholland in the Cahuenga Pass."

Celeste followed his directions and eventually merged onto the 101. As she drove, they talked about the strategy they'd use at Mariam's house—what they'd talk about, and how Truman might create an opportunity to poke around. The navigation app led them on the same roundabout exit onto Mulholland that Rolán had used. Cruising the winding hilltop road provided some dramatic glimpses of the basin below.

When they pulled into the familiar driveway, Truman leaned forward to get a look at the house in the daylight. It was Tudor-inspired, with a sharp pitched roof and dark beams in the white stucco. But it was incongruously huge for the style, on two floors, with lots of windows. It was a grand house, and it was hard to date it, but it didn't look new.

"That's Mariam's car," he said, gesturing to the Lexus. "Davo's isn't here."

"How do you know their cars?"

"Rolán pointed them out. He said they don't have a garage, so it's easy to tell whether they're home or not."

They climbed out and walked toward the front door. As they approached, Mariam stepped out, beaming at them. She was dressed for business, in a floral top and a black skirt.

"Welcome," she said, and waved them inside.

The foyer had a glittery chandelier, and a flight of stairs leading up, and a polished marble floor. That's what she wanted to do to his loft, Truman realized. It made the place look like an ice rink.

"This is a lovely home," Celeste said.

"Thank you. We work hard for it."

Mariam led them into a sitting room, with a Persian carpet, and dark wood furniture, and a lengthy overstuffed sofa and chairs. The coffee table in the middle was piled with thick fabric-sample books.

"Before we get started, Can I get you a coffee?" Mariam said.

They both declined, and Celeste said, "Do you have staff?"

"Not full-time." She waved them to the sofa. "Just cleaners who come in sometimes, and a cook a few mornings a week. Nobody on the weekend. But I do know how to make coffee."

Once they were seated, she stepped in front of Truman and sat between them, reaching for one of the heavy sample books.

"I thought we could start with the material for the curtains around the bed. My vision is that it should be a zone of mystery and seduction."

Celeste leaned closer, caressing a swatch of gauzy fabric, then flipped to the next one. "So many choices."

"I assume you want to leave the redbrick," Mariam said. "It's a little industrial, but it's a good color."

"I like the bricks," Truman said.

"So imagine that the floor is a glamorous white, plus the redbrick. What color should the bed curtains be?"

"It needs to be warm, don't you think?" Celeste said.

Mariam flipped to a creamy orange fabric and slid her hand behind it. Her fingers were visible through the sheer material.

"Imagine your bride," Mariam said, eyeing Truman, "nude and standing behind a wall of this."

"Wow—that's intense." He ran his hand through his hair. It was just about the last thing he wanted to imagine.

He listened to Mariam talk about the fabric, and the mood the different colors would create. After a few minutes, he interrupted.

"Can you point me to the bathroom?"

"It's in the foyer," she said. "Go right, and you'll see it on the left side."

Truman rose and walked into the foyer, glancing into the room on the opposite side. It was dark, the drapes drawn, but he could see a big dining table and a sideboard. He eyed the staircase, and briefly considered going up. It was carpeted, so Mariam wouldn't hear him. But it was too risky. Once he was up there, it would be too easy to be overheard from below.

Next to the dining room was what looked like an office. Stepping inside, he flicked the light on. There was a side table stacked with paper and more sample books, and a desk, but the drawers weren't big enough to conceal a motorcycle helmet. But maybe in the file cabinet.

Pulling gingerly on the top drawer so as not to make any noise, he rolled it open, but there was nothing inside but paper. The bottom drawer was the same. Gently closing it again, he killed the lights and walked out. Mariam's voice was still audible in the distance.

The last doorway in the foyer was the bathroom, he saw, glancing into it, and then on the left came an archway into another living room.

It had lots of glass that looked out onto a pool deck. On the right side was the kitchen, and he walked into the huge space. The fridge was twice as wide as a normal one, and the range top was similarly restaurant size. An island ran down the middle of the room. There was lots of cabinet space, but Davo wouldn't have put a bloody helmet in here.

At the far end was an open doorway, and Truman hurried over to it and stepped inside. A pantry, with open shelves of cans and bottles and boxes of food. On the right was another door, and he stepped over to it and tried the handle. It swung open, revealing a step down into a room with a bare concrete floor.

Based on the size and shape, this must have been a single-car garage at one time, in an earlier incarnation of the house. Today there was no way to get a vehicle inside—the only other entrance was a regular pedestrian door with a pane of glass in the top half. Beyond it he could see greenery, maybe the hedge that ran along the side of the house.

One wall was lined with cabinets, and he pulled open the first one. More food, stacked like in a supermarket—bags of flour and sugar, bottles of wine, a stack of empty plastic leftover containers. The next cabinet had cleaning supplies, and the one next to it had no shelves, just a collection of mops and brooms. There was no sign of a helmet in any of them.

Truman gently closed the last cabinet and turned to walk out. Next to the doorway, bolted to the concrete, sat a squat black safe. He hadn't noticed it when he'd walked in. It looked old, with a mechanical dial and a brass handle. No way would it be open, he thought. But he had to try. Grasping the handle, he gave it a twist, surprised that it rotated freely. After a quarter turn the internal mechanism made a dull *thunk*. When he gave it a tug, the door noiselessly swung open.

For a moment he paused to listen, gazing back into the pantry, but the only sound was his own pounding heartbeat.

Inside the safe were two shelves—on the bottom one was a heavy canvas bag, slender and black, like the ones he and Celeste used to store their cash. Its zipper was open, and Truman felt inside it. The bag was empty. On the top shelf was a lone business-size envelope. Something was written on it in blue ballpoint. He picked it up to read it:

Hwd Stg hq.

The envelope wasn't sealed, and when he opened the flap, inside he found a dull brass key. It looked too small to fit a regular door, but it had a manufacturer's logo on it. Pulling out his phone, Truman snapped a close-up photo of it, then photographed the writing on the front.

It was starting to feel like he'd been away too long. He quickly put the key back in the envelope, and set it on the shelf where he'd found it, then pushed the heavy safe door closed and walked back through the pantry into the kitchen.

As he passed the big double sink, Mariam appeared at the other end, stepping in from the foyer. Her brow furrowed when she caught sight of him.

"Did you find the bathroom?"

"I did," he said, and flashed a smile. "I came to get a glass of water."

"You don't have to drink out of the tap." She stepped up to the refrigerator, and pulled it open, and handed him a little green bottle of mineral water. "Try this." She took another with her as they walked back to the front room. As she approached the sofa, she offered the bottle to Celeste.

"Do you want to see the colors we picked?" Celeste said.

"Of course," Truman said, and sat with them.

They spent a minute looking at the fabric books, with Truman feigning interest in the lurid textures and colors. Eventually Mariam folded them closed.

"Before we order materials, the next step is to send my guys to your loft to measure everything."

"I'm a little worried about the cost," Truman said. "We haven't talked about that yet."

"We'll get to that," she said, and smiled. "Now—cocktails?"

"It's not even noon," Celeste said. "It'll have to be something light."

"How about a gin and tonic?"

"You read my mind."

Mariam rose and went to the far end of the room. There was a bar there, Truman saw, fronted by puffy leather upholstery, like in an old-school steak house. A trio of stools were finished in the same material.

They followed her over, instinctively climbing onto the barstools, and watched as Mariam made three gin and tonics.

"Go easy on the sauce," Celeste said. "I have to drive down that hill."

Mariam nodded and dutifully went light on the gin. She even had half a lime in the bar fridge to cut up and put on the rim.

"Cheers," she said, sliding them each a high-ball glass.

"This is such a great house," Truman said, tapping his glass against theirs. "The kitchen is the size of my whole loft."

"Not quite," Mariam said, and smiled. She

spread her palms on the bar. "It was built by an old film industry family before there were rules about the house-to-lot ratio—our land is mostly house. We don't even have room to build a garage. Davo and I have only been here about ten years."

"What does your husband do?" Celeste said, swirling the contents of her glass.

"He's an importer. Mostly Asian furniture."

"Do you have children?"

"Grown and moved out. Our son is studying in the Northeast, and our daughter is in DC."

"You said the decorating business is new," Celeste said. "Are you doing it because you're an empty-nester?"

"That might be part of it. I also needed something to do because Davo is so busy. His work, and he's politically active."

"In local politics," Truman said, "or in Sacramento?"

"He's involved in Armenian causes overseas." She waved a hand. "We're Armenian."

"Have you been there?"

"Davo has. There's always some intrigue. Since the Cold War ended, half the time it's a war zone. Even before that, our people have been screwed, chewed, and barbecued for centuries." She gestured with her glass. "Excuse my language."

"Can you speak Armenian?" Truman said.

"Davo is better at it than me. But I can manage."

They chatted some more, and finished the drinks, and eventually Celeste rose.

"Thanks for your hospitality."

Mariam stepped around the bar. "You and I should talk about art."

"When are you free?"

"How about tomorrow?" she said. "Do you go to church?"

"Oh, god, no."

"I might have a commitment in the morning, but if not, I'll text you."

At the front door, she grasped Truman's hand, thanking him with a sweet smile, and then exchanged an air kiss with Celeste.

Once they'd climbed into the little blue car, Celeste started the engine, and Truman pulled on his seatbelt.

"You got kisses," he said, "and I got a handshake. What's up with that?"

"I'd say it's because you're a client, but I'm a colleague. Also, your fiancée was standing right there."

Truman chuckled. "Got it."

"I tried to keep her talking," Celeste said, nosing the car out onto the street, "but she really wanted to go check on you. Did you get busted?"

"She found me in the kitchen. I think she was

a little suspicious, but I just said I was looking for water." He told her about the safe and the envelope with the key.

"That doesn't sound especially useful," she said, "if you don't know what the key is for."

"It was in the safe, though, right? That means it has to be something important. I have to try to decipher the squiggly writing. I assume it's Armenian script."

"But you didn't find a motorcycle helmet."

"Nothing like that. Even so, this feels like progress."

SIX

CELESTE GOT BACK ON the freeway and drove to Truman's loft. When she pulled up out front, she killed the engine and popped the door handle.

"You're coming up?" Truman said.

"We've got research to do."

"Right on. You're not working today?"

"Not at the gallery."

She grabbed her handbag from the backseat and followed him upstairs. At the purple sofa she pulled out her tablet, and kicked off her shoes, and sat with her back against the armrest. Truman grabbed his laptop and sat on the adjacent sofa.

It wasn't hard to find the manufacturer of the brass key, and Truman soon determined that it was meant for a padlock. Reading about how they were designed, it seemed the mechanism was similar to door locks. That meant his new lock-picking kit would definitely work—if he knew where Davo's padlock actually was.

"Do you want to hear about the Armenians?" Celeste said.

Truman set his laptop aside. "Sure."

"Mariam wasn't overstating it. There's a long history of them getting shoved off their land. The Ottomans tried to kill them all during World War I."

"Gross."

"Not just the Armenians. They went after the Greeks too."

"What is wrong with people?"

"Our species is infuriating. Even today they're under siege. I'm sure that's why Davo got involved with the Armenian cause."

On his phone, Truman pulled up the photo of the envelope and handed it to her. "I'm looking at the Armenian writing system. I'm pretty sure those are two letters, pronounced "ee" and "g." Maybe they're initials."

"I wonder why he'd write some of it in Latin letters and some of it in Armenian?"

"I only speak one language, so I'm sure I don't know. Do Spanish speakers do that? Mash them together?"

"Maybe." Celeste studied the image on the

screen. "The 'Hwd' might mean 'Hollywood.'"

"Or Howard, or Heywood."

"I wonder if the 'Stg' means 'stage'?" She handed the phone back. "Do you remember that girl who had the locker next to mine in eleventh grade? Lots of curly black hair. She was Armenian."

"Sure," Truman said. "Stacy or Suzie or something like that."

"Sosi. I ran into her a while ago. Her family runs a print shop in that mall on Seventh Street. I walked in to make some photocopies and she was working the counter. Maybe we can ask her if those initials mean anything."

Truman had to grin. "Great idea."

It took Celeste a minute to look up the number for the shop, then she pulled out her phone and dialed.

"Is Sosi working today?" she said, and a moment later ended the call and eyed Truman. "She'll be in this afternoon."

"It's not far." He folded his laptop closed. "Let's go talk to Sosi."

"First, can I make a withdrawal?"

"Let's do it."

Truman rose and walked over to his clothes rack and wheeled it out from the wall. Folded up behind it, leaning against the bricks, was an aluminum stepladder, and he carried it over next to the bathroom and pulled it open. Climbing up a few steps, he could see the top of the bathroom wall that he and Ernesto had built. Several short wrenches, each with a cord tied to it, spanned the gap between the drywall on the inside and the outside. He reeled one up, hand over hand, eventually producing a narrow canvas bag. Once he'd unclipped the carabiner that held it to the cord, he tossed the bag down to Celeste.

"These are getting dusty," she said, and set the bag on the floor, and pulled open the heavy zipper.

Packed inside were elastic-bound bundles of cash, a mix of twenties and hundreds, that they had taxed from a couple of drug dealers on Truman's first case. Both guys had wound up in prison, and as far as those lowlifes knew, the police had confiscated their money.

Celeste counted out a sheaf of bills, then looked up at him. "Do you need some scratch?"

"Get me three grand."

She pulled off his cash, then wrapped the elastic around what was left of the bundle and zipped it back into the bag. Handing it up to Truman, she watched as he lowered it into the space between the sheets of drywall again, carefully setting the wrench so that it spanned the gap but couldn't be seen from either side.

"It's kind of amazing that no one has missed it," she said.

"I'm sure some drug boss did." Truman climbed down the ladder. "I wasn't sure we'd be able to spend it slowly enough not to attract attention, but I think we're managing."

"At this point it's about not running so much of it through the banks that it alerts the tax people."

Truman folded the ladder and carried it over to the far wall, leaning it against the bricks and then rolling his clothes rack in front of it. When he came back, Celeste handed him his wad of bills.

"I still wake up sometimes with my heart pounding," Truman said, "thinking Jaime will come looking for this."

"He has no clue that we took it. Plus he's in the hoosegow indefinitely. Even so, was it worth all the stress?"

He flapped the cash, fanning out the bills. "Hell, yeah. It took the pressure off constantly having to hustle for jobs."

"I have to agree. It's nice not to be broke all the time."

Once Truman had tucked some of the cash into his pants pocket, and the rest into his desk drawer, he followed Celeste down the stairs, and they climbed into her car. The mall had parking underneath, but Celeste spotted a street space out front and pulled in. Truman fed some quarters into the meter, and they went inside.

The print shop was a small storefront with signs in the window that said PHOTOCOPIES and PASSPORT PHOTOS. As they stepped in, an electronic chime sounded, and a woman came out of the back.

"Sosi," Celeste said.

Sosi greeted her with a smile of recognition. She had a mane of wild dark hair with a pair of red-framed eyeglasses perched on her forehead.

"I remember you," she said, eyeing Truman.

"Of course. It's been a while."

"I see you've filled out." She gave him the once-over. "They used to call you 'Gazelle.'"

"That's one of the kinder labels." He grinned. "At least I could outrun those football guys. They also used to call me 'Metal Mouth.'"

Sosi laughed. "I remember—you had braces. Bullies are so imaginative. I was 'Four Eyes' for four years."

"Right now you look fabulous," Celeste said, "with the glasses or without."

"Back at you, girl. What do you two need today?"

"We had a question about the Armenian language," Celeste said. "Can you read it?"

"Not well. I can try. If I get stuck, we can ask my uncle."

Truman pulled out his phone and showed her the photo of the text on the envelope.

"I'm not sure how the Latin letters relate," Sosi said, "but that's a number."

"Not letters?" Truman said.

"They're both. Like how Roman numerals work. It's the number twenty-three."

"I'm so glad we asked," Truman said.

He tucked his phone away, and they chatted with Sosi for a few minutes, until a customer walked in, setting off the door chime.

Celeste thanked her, and they stepped out.

On the drive back to Truman's place, she spotted a taco cart on the sidewalk, and pulled over just past it, parking in the red zone with her flashers on long enough for them to climb out and get a quick meal.

Once they were upstairs in his loft, Celeste said, "Show me that envelope again."

Truman grabbed his laptop, and found the photo, and set it on the coffee table. They sat together on the sofa to study it.

"If it's short for 'Hollywood stage,'" Truman said, "maybe it means stage 23, like the sound stages at a movie studio."

"Why would Davo need a key to that?" Celeste said. "Why would he even be going to a studio?"

"Maybe he's delivering furniture that they use on the sets."

"So why keep the key at home?" She furrowed

her brow. "You know, the 'Stg' could mean storage, like a self-storage place. Storage unit number 23."

"Storage units have padlocks on them, so that fits," Truman said, and sat forward. "It could also explain why he didn't write the whole thing in Armenian. 'Hollywood Storage' is the name of the business."

"Why would Davo need a storage unit when he has a whole warehouse?"

"Maybe he has something he wants to keep hidden from his employees and from his wife. Like a bloody motorcycle helmet."

Celeste reached for the laptop and did a web search. "There's only one business called Hollywood Storage. It's not in Hollywood, though—it's in North Hollywood."

Before Truman could peer at the map, the door buzzer sounded, and he got up and went to the talk box to answer. A deep voice came through the static, but the words were unintelligible.

"I'm coming down," Truman shouted, and then stepped out and trotted down the stairs.

A minute later he walked in again, carrying a cardboard box.

"What did you order?" Celeste said.

"A speaker to connect to my phone. So I can play music at better sound quality than what comes through my laptop."

He set it on the kitchen counter and dug in the drawer for a box cutter. The blade made quick work of opening the package, but the device was packed in white Styrofoam, and when he pulled it out, tiny bits of it billowed around, drifting in the air and falling to the floor like snow. As he unwrapped the speaker, more bits blew off.

"Why is this stuff disintegrating?" he demanded.

"Science," Celeste said, watching him from the sofa.

"I'm taking all this packaging out to the Dumpster before it gets worse."

Truman carried the empty packaging in front of him, with his arm extended, not wanting to get the airy white dots on his clothes, and headed out the door. When he got back, Celeste was at the kitchen counter, inspecting his new toy.

"Look at all this stuff," he said, swirling the Styrofoam detritus with his toe. "The little pieces are too light to be swept up. A broom will just disperse them farther around the room."

"It reminds me of a glitter bomb. You keep finding it for years."

"These little white dots are going to be all over this floor as long as I'm alive. Maybe even until the end of the universe."

"You could just buy a vacuum," she said.

"Maybe I'll let Mariam pave over it with her

white marble. Then at least they'll blend in."

"Don't you dare."

Truman's phone buzzed in his pocket, and he pulled it out to look. "It's Rolán," he said, and went back to the sofas.

"So I hear you took a deep dive into Luis," Rolán said, when Truman answered.

"He told you that?"

"We're old friends. We talk about everything. What did you learn about Davo?"

"I got into his house," Truman said.

"How did you manage that?"

"His wife invited me. We're doing some business together."

"Did you get a chance to look around?"

"I found an office, and a storage room on the ground floor, and an old-school safe. I didn't get upstairs, but there was no sign of your helmet anywhere."

"Where's the safe?" Rolán said.

"Off the kitchen. In a room that looks like it was a garage at one time."

"Was it heavy-duty? Do you think a couple of guys could lift it?"

"It was bolted to the concrete floor." Truman frowned. Was he seriously considering stealing it? "It wasn't locked either."

"So what was inside?" Rolán demanded.

Truman hesitated before he spoke. "Nothing.

I assume that's why it was open."

"Damn it," Rolán snapped. "So you haven't really learned anything."

"That's not true. I think Davo might have a storage unit somewhere."

"Why would a guy with a whole warehouse and a big-ass mansion need a storage unit?"

"Think about it," Truman said. "It's where you'd put something you don't want anyone else to see."

"Where is this place? Do you know the unit number?"

"I haven't found it yet. I have more research to do."

"You're killing me, Truman. How difficult can it be?"

"I learned a lot," he said. "You should be thanking me. And you're definitely going to have to pay me."

Rolán scoffed. "Call me when you find the place."

Truman looked at the screen and frowned. The guy really had hung up on him.

"You don't trust your own client," Celeste said. She'd opened a bottle of Italian soda, and came over with it, and dropped onto the adjacent sofa.

"He hasn't paid me yet. I want to find out what's what before I tell him everything."

She nodded. "That's probably wise."

"Biff says the detective's job is collecting information, not gossiping like a laundress hanging out bedsheets, and not spreading details around like a drunk with a box of cheap cigars."

"You and that book," Celeste said, and chuckled.

"We should look in that storage unit."

"You want to break in? No way. You could go to jail."

"We won't leave any trace," Truman said. "We'll just have a look. It's not a crime if you don't take anything."

"That's so not true. You know there are cameras all over those self-storage places."

"Nobody watches the video unless there's a theft. We're not doing that, so nobody's going to look for us."

"How do you propose to get into the storage unit? It's going to be locked."

Truman sat forward. "The key in that envelope is for a standard padlock. That padlock has to be on Davo's storage unit. Ergo we know what kind of lock it is. I'm sure I can open it."

She frowned. "How?"

"Biff talks about lock-picking, so I bought a set of tools online."

"Are you kidding me?" Celeste demanded.

"I've tried it on a few locks. It's not that difficult, although sometimes it takes a few minutes.

It definitely requires a bit of finesse."

"No one could accuse Truman of lacking in finesse."

He jumped up and went to his desk to retrieve the toolkit. It was a thin black case, not much bigger than a wallet, and he zipped it open to show her the array of little implements.

"These are intense," she said, taking the case and looking them over.

"I watched some videos. It's not that complicated."

Celeste sighed. "I assume you're going to need a ride out there. Maybe I could drop you off, and you could go in alone. That way I could dodge the felony rap."

"If I'm on my own, I can just take the metro. It would be more fun if you came along."

She sipped at her soda and watched him for a moment, her brow furrowed in thought.

"How about this," she said finally. "We buy the same kind of padlock, and if you can open it, we'll roll out to the Valley and go to the storage place together."

Truman beamed. "That's a great idea."

"We could buy it from your boyfriend at that hardware store in Westlake."

"He's not my boyfriend. I also don't want him to tell Rolán what I'm up to. Those two are gossipy like laundresses."

"Is there a hardware store that's closer?"

"There's one right by the freeway." Truman rose and tucked the toolkit in his hip pocket.

Celeste dropped her bottle in the recycling and stepped out, waiting for Truman to lock up before they went down to her car. On the street the shops were closed and the shadows were growing long with the end of the day. Celeste flicked on her headlights and pulled away from the curb.

SEVEN

THE HARDWARE STORE WAS just a few minutes' drive, and when Celeste nosed into a stall in the parking lot, Truman climbed out.

"I'll be right back," he said, and strode toward the entrance.

While she waited, Celeste checked her phone, and found a message from Mariam. Before long she caught sight of Truman, walking out of the store with a little bag in hand.

When he climbed in, she said, "Mariam wants to meet me tomorrow morning. She wants to come to the gallery."

"It would be better if you could go back to her house and snoop around."

"It might be hard to do that when it's just

me," Celeste said. "But I also don't want her at the gallery."

"Tell her you can't get in there on Sundays."

"Good idea." Celeste thumb-typed the message, and a moment later Mariam's reply came. "She says I should come back to her place."

"You can ask her for a house tour. Scope out places where Davo might have stashed a helmet."

"Doesn't that sound suspicious? 'Hey, show me your closets and storage spaces.'"

"Maybe the opportunity will come up in the moment." Truman pulled a brass padlock out of the little bag. "This is the same brand as the key, but I wasn't sure of the size. There were a few of them. I think this one is close."

Celeste took it from him, and briefly looked it over, then snapped it closed. She pulled out the key and put the U-shaped shackle over her middle finger, holding it toward him over the console.

"Go to work."

"Hold it steady," Truman said, and arched his back to grab his toolkit from his pants pocket.

Working with a sharp little tool in each hand, he peered at the lock and inserted them, gently moving them around.

"You kind of have to get two of them working in concert," he said, "then twist them like a key."

Celeste watched him work, his brow furrowed in concentration. Eventually she spoke.

"It's taking too long. We can't be standing in front of a storage unit like this."

"Maybe I'm using the wrong pick."

He swapped one of the tools for another from the kit, and went back to work. A moment later the lock clicked open.

"Yeah," Truman said, his tone emphatic. "Finesse, baby."

"Impressive. Do you think you could do it any faster now that you have the right tool?"

"Set it up," he said, and waggled one of the little picks.

Celeste snapped the lock closed again and held the shackle tightly in her upturned fist. It took him a few minutes, twisting the tools with intent concentration, but he got the lock to snap open, more quickly than the first time.

"Piece of cake." Truman grinned and slapped the console.

"So let's set some limits to keep ourselves out of jail. One, if there are lots of people wandering around the place, we abort."

"Agreed."

"Two, if it takes longer than a couple minutes to open the thing, we abort."

Truman nodded. "That's totally reasonable. Let's go."

Celeste started the engine and headed onto the freeway, navigating the heavy Saturday evening traffic over the Cahuenga Pass into the Valley. Her phone directed her onto surface streets, into a quiet commercial neighborhood, and soon they rolled up on the self-storage place, with a lighted sign facing the street that said HOLLYWOOD STOR-AGE in big red letters.

"That's it," Truman said, gesturing at the side window as it rolled by. "You missed it."

"I'm not going to park inside. The cameras will totally record my plates. We'll walk back."

Halfway up the block she pulled into a street space, and they climbed out, and walked toward the place on the dark deserted sidewalk.

"It has a pedestrian gate, and one for cars," Truman said, eyeing the tall steel fence as they got closer. "I can't really break through those."

"Let's go see."

As the came up to it, the vehicle gate started to roll open. Inside a pickup waited to drive out, its headlights glaring through the steel bars. Without a word Truman stepped through the gap, past the pickup, not looking back.

"Very subtle," Celeste said quietly, close behind him.

"We have to act like we're supposed to be here. So head high, shoulders back."

"I don't see an office or anything. Just the stor-age units."

They were facing a concrete path that was just

wide enough for two cars. Lining both sides were rows of steel shutters in squat single-story buildings. The whole place was floodlit from above. The door to a unit halfway along the aisle was rolled up, with yellow light spilling out. A sedan was parked in front of it.

"These are single digits," Truman said, eyeing the numbers above the doors. "It must be in another row."

They walked to the end of the aisle, checking the numbers, then around the end of the building and into the next row. Here there were two vehicles in front of open units, one with cardboard boxes piled next to it. The guy who was loading them into the vehicle ignored them as they walked past.

"These are numbered in the teens," Celeste said quietly. "It has to be the next row."

They walked around the end and in the next aisle found unit 23. There was a vehicle here too, an SUV with its lift gate open, but it was farther down, and on the same side, and no one was in sight.

"As far as I can tell, there's only one camera on this row," Celeste said. "It's at this end."

"Can you stand with your back to it?"

She casually stepped into position to block the camera's view of the door. Truman pulled out his toolkit and squatted to examine the padlock.

"It's different," he said.

"The wrong size?"

"It's a different brand."

"Should we abort?" Celeste said, but he already had his toolkit open.

She took a breath to steady her nerves, watching as he manipulated the lock with the little tools in the blue-white glare of the overhead lights. She could see the sweat on his forehead.

"It's taking too long," she said finally. "Time to abort."

"I need a different tool," he said, and swapped the black pick for another. To Celeste's eye, they looked exactly the same.

"Are we sure this is even the right unit?" she hissed.

Truman didn't look up, engrossed in his task. "What's the number on it?"

"It's definitely marked 23."

"Are you certain Sosi told us that was the number on the envelope?"

"I'm positive." Celeste took another deep breath. Her heart was pounding. "I really think it's time to abort."

"I've almost got it."

"I'm going to start walking."

"Don't do that," he said. "Just one more second."

Celeste glanced over her shoulder, relieved

that at least no one was in view. At that moment she heard the lock click open.

"We're in," Truman said quietly.

He pulled off the lock, and rolled up the shutter door, and flicked on the light switch.

"Whoa," he said, taking in the space. Cardboard boxes were piled on top of furniture—a kitchen table, a low dresser, dining chairs. Narrow paths led among the stacks.

Celeste put her hand firmly in the middle of his back and shoved him inside, then pulled the shutter down, leaving a few inches of space at the bottom.

"Someone might lock us in," he said.

"No one's going to do that. You've got the padlock."

"Here's 'Christmas,'" Truman said, stepping farther in and reading the felt pen scrawled on the cardboard boxes. "And 'kid's clothes.' You could hide a helmet in any of these."

Celeste pulled open the top of a tall box that was sitting on the floor near the door. "They didn't even fold this stuff," she said. "They just dumped it in the box." She reached deeper, feeling around, but there was nothing in it but clothing.

"What do you suppose this is?" Truman said.

He was standing near the back, next to a bulbous pink device mounted on a metal stand. A thick canvas belt hung from it at waist level.

"It's an exercise belt," she said. "You put the belt around your butt, and the motor vibrates it at high speed, and the fat just melts away."

"That can't really work."

"You don't see them anymore, so I'd say you're right, it's useless."

"Why would Mariam keep it?"

"Maybe it's Davo's."

They both dug in the boxes, not even needing to cut through packing tape because they were just folded closed. Most of the boxes were small, and determining whether there was anything as bulky as a motorcycle helmet inside went quickly, a simple matter of opening the flaps to peer inside.

"Check this out," Celeste said. A white metal box sat on top of a battered credenza. "It's a tampon dispenser for a public restroom."

Truman stepped over and read the label. "'Sanitary protection.' I'm glad they're sanitary. I wouldn't use the other kind."

"It only takes nickels," she said. "I can't imagine how long ago a tampon would have cost that little."

"Everything feels dusty, and filmy," Truman said, opening another box. He really wanted to wash his hands. "This stuff feels like junk. Like someone didn't have any more room in their garage."

"Mariam said they didn't have a garage."

"I found a storage room, though. Next to the kitchen. It was a lot neater than this."

"Does this furniture look anything like what Mariam had in her house?" Celeste said.

"It's more like thrift-store stuff. Used but also cheap. Maybe they're newly wealthy, and this is from earlier in their marriage."

"She said they'd been in that house for ten years. Would they really keep the cheap stuff, and pay rent on it? Wouldn't they just donate it?"

Truman met her gaze. "You're thinking we broke into the wrong storage unit."

"Did you find a motorcycle helmet? I didn't see anything like that. And you said the padlock was different."

He groaned. "Let's get out of here."

Celeste rolled up the door and looked around outside. The unit that had been open earlier was locked up now, the vehicle gone, and the aisle was deserted. She stood with her back to the camera as Truman rolled the door down and snapped on the lock.

"This way?" he said. "It's shorter."

"We'd be walking right under the camera. Let's not provide a close-up if we don't have to. We'll go the long way."

"There are lots of other cameras," he said, following her toward the end of the row.

"Let's hope it's like you said: no one worries about them unless there's an incident."

Back at the street entrance, next to the driveway, Truman pushed open the crash door in the steel fence. Once they were out on the sidewalk, on the way back to the car, he took a deep breath.

"That was freaking weird. It's a relief to be out of there."

"Like a bad thrift store," Celeste said. "We were wrong about the place. Maybe we were wrong about all of it—wrong about what the writing on the envelope means."

She stepped around to the driver's side of her car, and they climbed in.

"High five," Truman said, once he'd closed his door, and held up his palm.

She slapped it, but frowned. "Why? We didn't find the helmet."

"We also didn't get arrested." He waved a hand. "And that was the first real-world use of my lock-picking tools."

"Felony break-in," she said, and started the engine. "Woo-hoo."

"We didn't do anything wrong."

"Legally we did, but maybe not morally. I'd say Biff Sturgis has guided you into the hard-nosed detective's gray area."

As Celeste flicked on her lights and pulled away from the curb, Truman looked out at the dark street. "I can't believe it's Saturday night and I don't have a date."

"You just bonked Rolán's friend last night."

"Sweet Luis." Truman sighed. "Last night wasn't Saturday, though. Tonight is Saturday."

"Are you going to see him again?"

"Probably. He's kind of hot."

"And that's the most important thing of all," she said, eyeing him sidelong.

"I know you're not being serious."

"Oh—brainwave," she said, braking for a red light.

"You sound like Mariam."

"Since we're already out here, we should go to that bar with the line dancing."

"I do like that place. Gay and Anglo without being a scene. Lots of eye candy."

"Do you remember where it is?" Celeste said.

"Isn't it on Ventura Boulevard?"

"That's, like, twenty miles long. I'll never find it. Driving in the Valley is like those old cartoons, where the background is on a loop of the same places. Gas station, supermarket, muffler shop, gas station …"

Truman pulled out his phone and tapped at the map on his screen. "It's not far. When you hit Ventura, turn right."

The place was already crowded when they stepped inside, and lots of the patrons on the dance floor were dressed Western, moving to the upbeat country-pop music. There weren't any seats at the bar.

Celeste leaned close to be heard over the music. "I'll push my way in. Margarita?"

"Do you remember there's a little bar upstairs?"

She nodded. "Let's try that one."

The room upstairs was quieter, and there were a couple of open stools for them at the bar. As the bartender stepped up, he greeted them with a smile.

Truman ordered his usual margarita, and Celeste asked for Jack on ice.

"It's so different here," she said, as the guy stepped away. "Like a small town."

When their drinks arrived, Truman pulled out cash to pay for them, and they clinked glasses. After the first gulp he wiped the salt off his lip.

"So I think we just broke into some stranger's hoard," he said.

"It definitely didn't feel like Mariam's stuff."

"The lock didn't match the key I found. I should have taken that as a red flag."

A guy sat on the barstool next to Celeste, and Truman checked him out. He had short hair, and a dark mustache, and a bit of paunch. Celeste turned briefly to see what he was looking at.

She raised her eyebrows. "Is it time for the irresistible dichotomy?"

"Engage," Truman said.

It was a tactic they used to hit on guys—they both flirted, and their target could choose either one of them, a theoretically irresistible offer. In practice, though, it didn't usually work.

Celeste shifted back, and they both swiveled toward him. Once he'd ordered a drink, he turned to look at them, sensing their attention.

"Hey," Truman said, echoed by Celeste.

The guy nodded.

"Do you like sriracha?" Truman said.

His eyes narrowed. "Who doesn't like sriracha? It's the god condiment. Why do you ask?"

"We're both equally curious," Celeste said.

"About hot sauce."

"It's the best condiment," she said.

"You two are sweet," he said, "but I'm not looking to hook up."

"Me neither," Truman said.

Celeste waved a hand. "I'm not either."

He laughed. "You just sit at the bar talking about sriracha?" The guy's drink arrived, and he paid for it, then got up. "Have a good night."

Celeste sipped her bourbon. "How boring."

"He must be one of those asexuals," Truman said. "We should dance."

They finished their drinks, and headed down the stairs, and spent some time on the dance floor. It felt good to move, Celeste thought, to sweat a little and blow off some of the stress that built up during that break-and-enter.

After a while Truman jabbed his thumb toward the entrance. His face was glistening with sweat, and he looked the way she felt: worn out but happy. Celeste nodded and followed him out to the street.

They rode back over the hill in comfortable silence. It felt good to be part of all the noise once in a while, Truman thought. To get some exercise and sweat a little. He knew he'd sleep well.

EIGHT

Her mother didn't work on Sunday, Celeste remembered, waking in the morning to the sound of her puttering in the house. She got up and went into the kitchen to pour herself a bowl of cereal.

María appeared, her dark hair pulled back, dressed for a day off in comfortable jeans. She poured them each a coffee, then sat across the kitchen table.

"You've been out late the last few nights," she said. "Is there a boy?"

"I went out with a guy on Friday," Celeste said, grasping the warm mug. "Last night Truman and I went dancing."

"Truman is the opposite of boyfriend material," María said. "What's this other one like?"

"I'm not sure yet. Blue-collar. Curious about the world. I don't know him very well."

"What kind of blue-collar?"

"Right now I think he's unemployed."

María sipped her coffee and frowned. "He doesn't sound like much of a catch. He should be working on finding a job, not chasing girls."

"I'll let him know you feel that way."

She chuckled at that, and they chatted for a while, until Celeste had to get ready to leave. Gray trousers and a plain top, she decided. That might project how serious she was about art.

In her jewelry box she found half a tab of Vicodin, and ground it into a paste between her teeth, grimacing at the bitterness. It was irresponsible, she knew, doing that right before a business meeting. But it wasn't enough to make her impaired, and it would mellow things out, take the edge off.

After she said good-bye to María, she went out to the driveway, and ran her tongue over her teeth to get rid of the chalky residue. Truman had figured it out, that she used opioids once in a while, and he'd confronted her about it. She'd promised him that she'd handle it, and taper off, and eventually quit. No way was she going to do any kind of twelve-step. Right now she was working on getting into the mind-set of quitting, and that meant it was already less of an issue.

The freeways were faster today, and the drive

on Mulholland went faster too, now that she was familiar with the route. When she pulled into the yard at Mariam's house, there was a dark-green sedan parked next to the gold Lexus.

Mariam pulled the door open when Celeste knocked, and welcomed her in. She was wearing another riotously colorful top.

"How about coffee?" she said.

"That sounds great."

Celeste followed her into the kitchen, where Mariam waved her to a high table with tall chairs, like in a bar. The coffee machine on the island counter was the kind that made one cup at a time with little plastic pods.

As Mariam set to work on it, Celeste glanced around the kitchen. It was a huge space. This house would be perfect to throw a party. The far end was where Truman had found the pantry and the safe, and on the other side of the foyer was a big open room with lounge furniture.

"Is that another living room?"

"It faces the pool," she said, focused on the coffee machine. "Take a look if you want."

Celeste stepped off the chair and walked over. Big glass sliders fronted the pool deck, a compact space with some patio furniture and palm trees around the inviting blue water. More interesting was the broad oil painting on the wall above the sofa. She stepped closer to take a look.

From the far end of the room a man stepped in, and paused when he caught sight of her, and stood up straighter. This had to be Davo. Wearing jeans and a taupe golf shirt, his hair was still thick and dark, even though he had to be in his fifties. Mariam was probably the same age, but it was hard to tell with her meticulous grooming. This guy wasn't bad looking, and had a bit of flab, but he was built thick, and looked strong.

"Good morning," he said, and flashed a smile.

"Mount Ararat," Celeste said, gesturing to the oil painting. "It's an artful rendition. Is that the way it looks from Yerevan?"

Davo's eyebrows shot up, and he rattled off a rapid string of words.

"I assume you're speaking Armenian," she said, and smiled. "I don't speak the language."

"Are you Armenian?" he demanded.

"I'm actually Latina, but I only speak English, much to the disappointment of my parents."

"So how do you know about Ararat and Yerevan?"

She shrugged. "I know the mountain is important. Especially as a national symbol."

Mariam appeared in the archway from the kitchen.

"I like this one," Davo said, eyeing his wife. "She knows something about the world."

Mariam introduced them, and they went

back into the kitchen. Celeste sat on the tall chair again, and Mariam brought two coffee cups to the table, sliding one to Celeste.

"I love your house," Celeste said. "You both must work hard."

"Not on Sunday." Davo laughed, and put his hands on his hips. "So you're an art dealer. Is that really a good painting of Ararat?"

"I work in a gallery, so I'd call myself a curator more than a dealer. 'Good' is subjective. I can tell you the artist is a professional, and the technique they used is hard work. Getting that level of detail with brushes is time-consuming."

Davo nodded. "You can get paintings wholesale for Mariam's business?"

"My markup will be less than a gallery would charge," Celeste said. "The most important thing I can offer is that I'm dialed in to the local art scene, so I know where to source artworks."

"I'm redoing the loft she and her fiancé are moving into once they get married," Mariam said.

"Congratulations," he said. "What does your fiancé do?"

"He's mostly a consultant."

"In what field?"

"Logistics," Celeste said, trying to think quickly. She hadn't anticipated this—Truman was better at spinning the cover stories.

"That usually means shipping."

"He used to work for a company that designed packing materials for electronics. You know that white foam that's inside the box? It's so that if you drop it, the stuff inside won't break."

"So he designs packaging for consumers?" Davo said, his brow furrowing. "Like a delivery company? Or he designs packaging that ships from the factory?"

Celeste frowned, trying to look thoughtful. "I know he never worked in a factory. I'm not really sure of the details. You'd have to ask him."

"I'd like to meet your fiancé. I might have some work he could do."

"I thought you were an importer."

"I ship things locally once I get them here," Davo said. "To retail shops and designers. Maybe he could help."

"That's how I got started as a decorator," Mariam said. "Some of Davo's clients needed furniture for their offices and their houses. But they didn't know what else to put in the space, or what colors to use. I have a gift for that."

"Can I give you my number?" Davo said. "Have your fiancé call me."

"Of course." Celeste pulled out her phone and thumb-typed as Davo recited it.

"What's his name?"

"Truman," she said, meeting his gaze.

"I'll look forward to talking to him." He eyed

Mariam. "I'm going out for a while."

"Please tell me you're not going to work."

"It's just an errand," he said, and waved dismissively.

"Will you be back for lunch?"

"It's right off the freeway. I won't be long." Davo winked at Celeste and walked into the foyer.

Celeste heard the front door close as Mariam sipped her coffee.

"He's a handful, that one," Mariam said.

"He seems nice enough."

"I'm not sure what he's up to half the time. He says it's his political activities, but in the back of my mind I always wonder if it's another woman."

"Have you seen any evidence of that?"

"Zero," she said flatly. "That's why he still lives here."

Celeste laughed. "Men are generally a lot of work."

"Your man seems like a gentleman."

"He's not always the most rational person." She sat up straighter. "Enough about men. Let's talk business."

Mariam nodded. "I was thinking about my clients. I can put them in three categories: poster art, real art that's not expensive, and then prestige art."

Celeste explained the kind of artists she worked with, and the genres, and the price ranges.

They talked about Celeste's cut and how the acquisition process would work. Eventually they got the details hammered out.

"You know, I'm going to a design event this week," Mariam said. "It's downtown. You should come."

Celeste drained her cup. "What kind of event?"

"It's about women in design. In my industry and the fashion business. There are some seminars, but mostly it's about networking. It's not expensive. Monday and Tuesday at the furniture mart."

"I might have some time tomorrow," Celeste said, and stood up. "Send me the details."

Mariam walked her to the door and grasped her hands. "I'm excited about our collaboration."

"Let's make some money," Celeste said, and went out to the front yard.

The green sedan was gone now, she saw, as she climbed into her car. She twisted the key in the ignition, but before she pulled onto the street, she sent Truman a text:

News. Stop by the gallery later?

His terse reply came soon after: a lone thumbs-up symbol.

———·———

SAFFRON'S CAR WASN'T HERE, Celeste saw, as she parked behind the gallery. Stepping in through the fire exit, she turned off the alarm, then went to open the front door, and flipped the sign around to OPEN, and settled in at her desk.

A while later she was absorbed in reading emails when a couple of people walked in, a thin guy with a bushy Afro and a woman in a billowy summer dress. This wasn't Saffron's potential whale, Celeste realized, looking them over. These two were out exploring the neighborhood. They greeted her and then walked around to look at the canvases. Eventually the woman wandered back to her desk.

"Who's the artist?" she said.

"There are several." Celeste handed her a copy of the exhibition catalog. "This has some biographical details on them."

She flipped through it and frowned. "There are no prices listed anywhere."

"The range is fifteen to thirty," Celeste said, "and the large piece on the far wall is forty-five."

"Hundred?" she said.

"Thousand."

She carefully set the catalog on the desk. "We're not really in the market."

"That doesn't mean you can't enjoy the art. Take your time with it."

The woman thanked her, and the pair of them wandered around a little longer, and eventually left.

When the potential client stepped in, Celeste recognized her at a glance. They'd never met, but she looked like a dentist—her mousy brown hair neatly parted and tucked back, wearing capri pants and a logo-branded plaid shirt that a stylist would have told her looked suitably casual for her day off.

"Dr. Larsen," she said, and rose.

"That sounds so serious," the woman said, and smiled. "Just call me Andrea."

"I'm Celeste. Saffron said you'd drop in today. Can I offer you a mineral water?" She shook her head, and Celeste stepped around the desk. "Let me introduce you to what's on display."

———◆———

TRUMAN PULLED ON A pair of chinos and a polo shirt and set off walking toward the Arts District. It was warm today, and he enjoyed the sunshine. When he got close to Celeste's gallery he stopped at a coffee place and bought two espressos, then carried them up the block to the white facade that bore sleek metal letters that read SAFFRON SWATI GALLERY.

When he stepped inside, Celeste was standing at the back, talking to a woman. Celeste's outfit was somber, gray trousers and a light blouse, probably intended to lend gravity to her role as an authority on the art.

The pair of them were facing a painting that looked like angry black smudges on an oversize metal sheet. It was supposed to be a cat, maybe, with ferns and shrubbery growing out of its chest, but from a distance it looked more like the kitchen foil on a baked potato that had been in the oven too long. Celeste was gesturing with both arms, and the woman stood with her feet apart, arms folded. Truman set the espresso cups on the front desk and stood nearby, absently staring at a canvas and straining to overhear their conversation.

"It's so dark," the woman was saying. "It feels overwhelming. Almost oppressive."

"Then the artist has succeeded," Celeste said. "Life isn't just about happy things, Andrea. Everyone loves blue skies and puppies and ice cream, but there's more to it."

"I'm worried that my patients will find it a little heavy."

"They'll also see that you're not afraid of having a serious conversation about the world. That you can engage honestly with the human condition, and look it in the eye, regardless of the discomfort."

"I guess that's true. I'm just not sure I like it."

"It doesn't matter whether you like it or not," Celeste said. "It goes way beyond you. What matters is that you're willing to be bold, and not afraid, and face life on its own terms, even if that makes you uncomfortable from time to time."

"This painting says all that?"

"Hanging in your office, it certainly will."

"I'll have to think about it," she said. "Maybe don't sell it to anyone else for a few days. Just until I figure it out. Can I take a photo of it?"

"I can do better than that. The exhibition catalog has an excellent color reproduction of it."

Celeste stepped over to her desk and handed her a copy of the booklet.

"Thanks for explaining everything," she said.

"Of course." Celeste walked her to the door. When she closed it behind her, she eyed Truman and said, "Phew."

"One of your whales?" he said.

"Saffron called her a small whale."

"Is she going to buy that dumpster fire of a painting?"

"Fifty-fifty. If she balks I'll just advise her to wait for the next exhibition. We'll do something lighter next time."

Truman gestured to her desk. "I brought you an espresso."

Celeste sat down and reached for the paper cup, taking a sip. "Thanks—this is delicious."

"It doesn't matter whether you like it or not," Truman said, dropping into the chair across from her. "It goes way beyond you."

She laughed at that. "It sounded better when I said it."

"How was Mariam today?"

"I think we'll be able to do some work together," she said, and explained how she planned to help Mariam acquire art.

"I hope it won't mess up your business relationship when I blow off the decorating gig."

"We're going to have to do that tactfully."

"I'm not in a rush," Truman said.

"But we will have to nip it in the bud before she sends workers to measure your loft for materials."

"We could tell her we had a blowout fight, and threw dishes at each other."

"Then she'd just convince you that you needed to redecorate to cheer yourself up."

"Hmm." Truman furrowed his brow. "We could tell her that you decided you don't want to live there. The neighborhood is too gritty. We're looking for another place."

"Much better," Celeste said. "That leaves it open-ended."

"I had no idea the hetero world could be so complicated. From the outside it just looks bland and boring. Minivans and white bread and tan chinos."

"You wear tan chinos," she said. "By the way, I set up a meeting for you with Davo."

"That's great. You met him?"

"He was at the house. I figured if you talked to the man himself you might be able to get a better perspective on Rolán's problems."

"What kind of vibes did you get from him?" Truman said.

"He seems pretty regular. I'd say Old World masculine."

"What does that mean, exactly?"

"He talks loud, and takes up a lot of space, but he's not aggressive."

"What's the reason I'm going to meet him?"

Celeste explained what Davo had said, then pulled out her phone. "I'll text you his number."

"Thanks for setting it up. It's amazing that I can go talk to him." He set his cup on the desk. "The only problem is that I don't know anything about that field. Where did you come up with shipping and packaging?"

"I had to invent something fast," she said. "I was thinking about your Styrofoam dots problem. You were practically in a crisis over it yesterday. I was pretty vague about it with Davo—you can always tell him your skill set doesn't apply to his ask."

He nodded. "I'll make it work. I'll have to do some reading."

NINE

B ACK AT HOME, TRUMAN grabbed his computer and stretched out on one of the sofas. Shipping and packaging, it turned out, were not a straightforward matter. People went to engineering school for years to learn about it. The ISO had hundreds of pages of documented standards for boxes and other containers, and lots of guidelines about how things were supposed to be transported.

First he read about what the ISO was—the International Organization for Standardization. Headquartered in Geneva, it set standards in dozens of industrial fields. Even though that sounded important, he'd never even heard of it. Next he dug into some of the academic material, and read about crush resistance, and displacement, and how to calculate the cost of protecting the payload. Even a few millimeters of extra padding in a box could add several dollars to the wholesale cost of the product.

Eventually he couldn't read anymore, and folded his laptop closed, and took a deep breath. Pulling out his phone, he dialed Davo's number, surprised that he answered.

Truman introduced himself, and added, "Celeste said I should call you."

"You're a lucky man," Davo said. "She's beautiful."

"Thanks," he said, and frowned. "So what can I help you with?"

"I understand you work in packaging design."

"That's right," Truman said. "I specialize in minimizing displacement and unnecessary wasted space in padding material."

"Exactly what I need help with. Are you a nine-to-six type or a consultant?"

"I mostly work on my own."

"So you'll come to my warehouse," Davo said. "We'll discuss my problem."

"I can do that. It can't hurt to talk."

"Tomorrow after lunch?" Davo said, and rattled off his address.

Once he'd ended the call, Truman sat there absently gazing out the tattersall windows. They were set too high for a view of the neighborhood, but he could see a broad swath of blue sky. Hopefully he could bluster his way through this meeting with Davo.

—◦—

THE GALLERY WAS QUIET again after Truman had left. Saffron didn't like to have music on, as she said it detracted from the visual experience, but sometimes Celeste blasted it anyway when no one else was here. She was thinking about doing that when her phone buzzed—it was Rolán.

She smiled as she picked up. "It's the carjacker."

"Hey—I asked you politely for a ride."

"I guess that's mostly true."

"Listen, all those vegan food trucks are on York Boulevard tonight. Do you want to go explore?"

"That sounds like fun. Shall I meet you over there?"

"I thought we could go for a bike ride on the way," he said. "There are some great lookout spots around Elysian Park."

"You want me to sit on the back of your motorcycle?" she said.

"It's totally safe. I've been riding since I was twelve."

"Oh, man." She took a breath. It sounded dangerous, but thinking about it, it also sounded kind of hot. "Maybe if it's just from downtown to

Highland Park. That's not too far, right?"

"You're going to love it."

———•———

TRUMAN WAS READING ABOUT packaging again when his phone buzzed.

When he picked up, Rolán said, "What did you find out about the storage unit?"

"Unfortunately there isn't one," Truman said, sitting up and setting his computer aside. "It was a false lead."

"Are you shitting me?" he demanded. "What a waste of time."

"These things don't happen instantly. It's part of the research. My next step is to go meet Davo."

"Why would you do that?" Rolán said, his voice rising.

"Why not? His wife introduced us. It's an opportunity for me to interview him."

"Don't do that. It's a bad idea."

"It's actually a great opportunity," he said. "And it's already set up."

"What the fuck, man? I didn't tell you to talk to Davo."

Truman frowned. "I don't understand why this is a problem. If he's still got your helmet, maybe I can figure out where he stashed it. I'm not going to ask him point-blank, if that's what you're worried about." He took a breath. "There's also the thing where you don't get to tell me what to do if you don't pay me."

"Listen," Rolán said. "If you really have to meet with him, at least don't tell him I know you. And don't ask him about me."

"I'm not new at this, Rolán. I can collect information from someone without telling them what I know."

"All I really need from you is the layout to his house."

"Let me do my job," Truman said. "I'll call you when I know more—and you can bring me some money. And don't go up there and try to break in. It didn't work out very well the last time."

Once he'd ended the call, Truman walked over to his bedside table and grabbed the *Hard-Nosed Detective* book, then went back to the sofas. If he was going to interview Davo tomorrow, he needed to refresh his memory. He found the section titled "How to Grill a Patsy without Tipping Your Hand" and read through it, then set the book aside and spent more time reading online about packaging and displacement.

The flaky disintegrating Styrofoam that still swirled around his floor was actually a technical advancement in the field, he learned. It was cheaper and had better crush resistance, so manufacturers could use less of it to ship electronics from Asia, and that significantly reduced transportation costs.

Clicking around from page to page, he read that the concept of displacement was also related to engines. It was a basic measure of engine size and corelated directly to power. Reading about it felt tangential, as it wasn't really about packaging and shipping, but it was interesting, and he got distracted with all the details of pistons and cycles and engine power.

When his phone buzzed sometime later, he was glad for the interruption. It was Luis, he saw, and picked up.

"Do you want to do something tonight?" Luis said. "There's an event I want to go to. Do you know where Boyle Heights is?"

"I may have heard of it," Truman said, his tone sharp.

"Don't get steamed. Anglos aren't always aware of anything outside the white neighborhoods. Do you know how many blond girls have told me, 'I never go east of La Brea unless I'm in an airplane headed to New York'?"

"I'm not blond," Truman said. "You know where I live. It's not exactly the affluent Westside."

"So you're a homie. I get it."

He took a breath, and resisted his instinct to react to that. "What time does this event start?"

"Don't you want me to tell you about it first?" Luis said. "That way you can decide if you want to go."

"You're interested in whatever it is, right? That's good enough for me."

"You don't actually know me that well."

"Will I have to do anything that's very physical," Truman said, "or embarrassing? Help build a house, or pick trash out of the river, or sing in front of a crowd?"

Luis laughed. "Nothing like that."

"Will my clothes get wet? That's not a total deal-breaker. I can handle a splash of water or juice from a stomped tomato. I just won't wear light-colored pants."

"No liquids will be thrown at you."

"So that's all I need to know. I'll probably enjoy it more if I don't know anything about it."

————◆————

CELESTE DIDN'T WANT ROLÁN to know exactly where she worked, so she arranged to meet him at Pershing Square. She locked up a few minutes before the gallery's posted closing time and headed out. Saffron didn't mind—she said it added mystique to the place when it was inaccessible during business hours.

Climbing into her car, she drove to the square and down the ramp into the parking lot underneath. Before she got out, she dug in the console and found half a Vicodin, crunching it between her teeth. Good thing she'd worn trousers today, she thought, climbing the stairs to the street.

She stood on the sidewalk, and it wasn't long before a motorcycle pulled up, its rider clad in a familiar leather jacket and a black helmet. Rolán kicked the stand down and lifted his tinted visor, flashing her a smile. He twisted around to pull a helmet off the back and handed it to her.

"Climb on," he said.

"Not so fast. I need a lesson first on how not to fall off."

"There's a footrest for you on either side," he said, pointing one out. "The safest stance for you is to put your hands on my waist, and lean into me on the turns."

"OK, but no wheelies, no burnouts, and no slamming on the brakes."

Rolán laughed. "I'll do my best."

When Celeste pulled on the helmet, she was surprised at how comfortable it was. It even allowed for peripheral vision. Gingerly swinging her knee over the seat, she put her shoes on the footrests, and got comfortable, then put her hands on his waist, gripping Rolán's jacket.

As they started rolling, she inhaled sharply. Her heart was pounding. When the bike changed course it felt more like an amusement park ride than riding a bicycle, and it was nothing like driving a car. When Rolán turned a corner, she leaned close to him. It was kind of intuitive, she realized—her body followed his, and his was in tune with the bike.

He accelerated onto the freeway, but just for a few blocks, and then exited at the stadium. There was nothing happening there, and the roads around it were quiet. Rolán drove on the hilly winding streets around Elysian Park. He was right: there were some great views of downtown, the office towers and the sprawling hazy basin, with the sun behind it all, low in the west.

By the time they got down the other side of the hill, cruising the streets toward Highland Park, Celeste's apprehension had faded, and she was starting to enjoy the ride. Rolán turned onto York, and she saw that the food trucks were already here, spaced along the boulevard, a few on each block. Lots of people were walking around, and some were eating, either perched on temporary benches or standing on the sidewalk.

Rolán pulled into a street spot, and set the kickstand, and killed the engine. Once Celeste had stepped off the bike, she pulled off the helmet and adjusted her hair.

"That was more fun than I thought it would be."

He grinned. "I'm glad. You did great."

She gestured across the street. "I propose that our first stop is that mac-and-cheese truck."

TEN

W HEN TRUMAN'S PHONE BUZZED, he rose from the sofa to pull it out of his pants. Luis's text was brief:

Here.

Truman was already dressed, in dark chinos and a lustrous shirt with an orange and yellow paisley print. He usually wore it to dance clubs, but since he didn't know where they were going, he had no idea what he should wear.

When he got down to the street, Luis was standing at the driver's door of his funky old Pacer, looking across the vehicle. Beretta stood nearby on the sidewalk. They were chatting, Truman realized. Beretta nodded to him, then walked into the alley. Luis got in behind the wheel and reached across to unlock the passenger door.

"Your friend Beretta wondered if I needed security on my car again this evening," he said, starting the engine and pulling away from the curb.

"He's more of a neighbor than a friend."

"I told him I might need his services later tonight."

Truman laughed. "I admire your foresight."

"I think he knows you're gay," Luis said. "He called me 'sweetheart.'"

"Beretta has boundary issues."

"I wondered if it was because you have a constant stream of male visitors."

"Nope. I'm not that guy."

Luis navigated toward the freeway ramp, not using a navigation app and not asking for directions, as if he already knew the neighborhood. He drove fast but calm, and cruised as far as the big interchange in East LA, and exited onto surface streets in Boyle Heights.

This neighborhood was always tight for parking, but he found a street space along a leafy green park. Across the street was a sprawling building with a mostly dried-out lawn. A dozen people were standing around, near a table set up out front, and more were walking up.

"This used to be a hospital," Truman said, surveying the building as they climbed out. Facing west, it was bathed in the golden light of the end of the day.

"There's a plan to rehab it for housing. Right now it's empty. I guess that's why they let the grass die."

As they crossed the street and got closer, Truman admired the soaring facade. "Such a beautiful era for architecture."

"When was it built?"

"In the 1920s. The style is called art deco."

Luis gestured toward the table, where a trio of people sat with a laptop and a cash box, taping bright-pink wristbands on the new arrivals. They joined the line.

"Do you want me to tell you what we're doing here?" he said.

"No need. I'll find out soon enough."

When they got to the front, Luis gave them his name, and they each got a wristband. They followed the stream of people to the front entrance and into the building's lobby. The hospital reception counter and the waiting-room seating and the signage were all intact, but it looked worn, and the vibe was distinctly 1970s, likely the last time it had been renovated.

"I don't hear any music," Truman said, "so I know it's not a rave."

Luis chuckled and laced his fingers with Truman's as they walked. A staffer sent them down the hallway, and soon they emerged into a big industrial space, a maze of worn pipes and ducts and wiring. The boiler room, Truman realized, taking it in. A squat rusting furnace dominated the middle. The ceiling was twice the height of his loft. Another staffer directed them up a flight of metal stairs onto a catwalk, and they stopped halfway along the room, and stood at the railing with the string of other spectators.

"The only thing I can think of is that we're going to watch them fire up a century-old boiler," Truman said.

"Do you really think all these people would have bought tickets for that?"

"So then we're going to watch someone clean it? Or paint it? Or disassemble it?"

Luis chuckled, and looped his arm around his waist. Being with this guy felt so easy, and natural, and comfortable. He leaned in and met his mouth.

———◆———

AFTER CELESTE AND ROLÁN had split an order of mac-and-cheese, they walked up the block to a vegan doughnut truck.

"I thought I'd have room to try six different things," Rolán said, "not just the one."

"It's great food, though."

"I still can't believe it was vegan." He eyed her sidelong. "You seem a little mellow tonight. Are you on something?"

Celeste scowled. "I'm not on anything. I had a long fricking day."

"I'm not judging you."

"There's nothing to judge," she said, raising her voice. "Except that I work hard."

"Christ, forget I said anything."

She scoffed and kept walking. At the corner, she stepped out of the stream of pedestrians and paused to take in a mural filling the wall of the building on the opposite side.

"I should probably know who that is," Rolán said, standing next to her and studying the image.

"It's Pancho Villa. He was a revolutionary hero in Mexico."

The portrait was lifelike, in black-and-white, probably modeled on the films he'd starred in. Surrounding his head and filling the background was an intricate swirling kaleidoscope of muted pastel colors.

"I could have done that," Rolán said, and folded his arms.

Celeste chuckled. "But you didn't."

"I remember. To be honest, there's no way I could ever do anything even remotely like that."

———·———

A STRING OF MUSICIANS filed into the boiler room, dressed in regular street clothes and carrying their instruments—a violin, a viola, a couple of horns, and a woman with either an oboe or a clarinet. More spectators had lined the catwalk on the opposite side of the big space, and others stood around the edges of the floor.

"We're here for a concert?" Truman said, watching the musicians take their seats below.

"The music is secondary. The main performers are up next."

Two men and two women appeared, striding into the space, all of them dressed casually, like they were on the way to the supermarket or the bank, except that they were barefoot. They stood with their backs to each other, facing the room, unmoving.

"OK," Truman said. "You can tell me what's going on now."

"They're dancers. From the dance department at my college."

The music started, and the crowd fell silent. The performers slowly started to move, stepping outward, their actions deliberate, elegant. Gradually they got more energetic, and one of the men threw one of the women up in the air. She grabbed hold of a fat pipe and swung herself up onto it, moving effortlessly, like a gymnast, then fluidly paced along the pipe and climbed onto a platform higher up.

Soon the others were up on the pipes and the

ducts, and all around the room. They made it look easy to leap from perch to perch. There were some tender moments between them, slow embraces and sweeping dips, and eventually the four of them were on the floor again, and took a bow.

Truman clapped and hooted with the other spectators, and soon they filed out onto the dry lawn. Luis pointed the way to his car, and they walked toward the street.

"That was really beautiful," Truman said. "Elegant and edgy at the same time."

"I'm glad you were into it. The great thing about dance events is that they're usually short. You can't perform with that kind of intensity for very long."

"Do you want to come over for a nightcap?"

"I'm not sure what that means," Luis said, stepping around to the driver's side of his car, "but I like the idea of coming over to your pad."

"I think it means a drink. In old movies they use it as code for hooking up."

Luis eyed him as they climbed in. "That, I'm definitely up for."

As Luis navigated back onto the freeway, Truman said, "So tell me about Rolán."

"You're doing some research for him, he told me."

"What's his family name?"

"Why?" Luis said. "Are you looking into him?

Why not ask him yourself?"

"I guess I could. But you could save me the phone call."

"It's Hernández."

"How do you know him?"

"We were friends at school. We grew up around Panorama City and Pacoima."

"There's some rough stuff happening out there," Truman said.

"Almost as rough as where you live," he said, eyeing him sidelong.

"I meant the street gangs."

"Rolán and I never got jumped into a gang. Lots of neighborhood kids did. It was inevitable that our friends were gangbangers."

"You're a philosophy student. Would you say your ethos is rough the way Pacoima is rough?"

"I haven't studied ethos yet," Luis said, and chuckled. He kept his gaze focused on the road. "Seriously, though, I'd say Rolán is rougher than me. The gay thing kind of insulated me from it."

———◆———

AT THE DOUGHNUT TRUCK, Celeste let Rolán pick out one to share, and they sat on a bench together to eat it. When they got up again, Rolán arched his back, grimacing as he stretched.

"My place is near here," he said. "We can even walk."

Celeste's eyes narrowed. "So that's why we came to this neighborhood."

"We could have a shot of tequila to counteract the vegan food."

Rolán moved closer, and put his hands on her hips, and leaned in to nuzzle her neck.

"Let's go," she murmured.

He briefly rested his arm on her back as they walked up the boulevard, then onto a side street that gradually sloped uphill. At a small house Rolán led her into the driveway, then down the narrow walk to the back. It was a duplex, Celeste realized, and Rolán's place was the rear unit.

Stepping inside, he flicked the lights on. They were in a tidy little kitchen. Stuck on the refrigerator door with magnets were a couple of colorful kids' drawings, so messy and indistinct that they could pass for abstract art.

"Do you have a roommate?" Celeste said.

"It's just me."

Before she could ask about the drawings, he stepped into the next room. It had a big television set, and a puffy leather sofa, and a bar cart parked against one wall. Rolán went to it and twisted open a bottle of tequila, then set out two shot glasses.

Wandering over to the coffee table, Celeste surveyed the array of magazines.

"Bottoms up," Rolán said, and held out a glass.

Celeste folded her arms. "Whose house is this?"

"I told you—it's mine."

"Whose art is on the fridge?"

He frowned. "My nephew's."

"And you read women's fashion magazines?" she demanded, and gestured to the table.

"All right," Rolán said, and sighed. "It's my sister's house, and my sister's kid. I live with my parents. I can't really bring a woman home. And I never get to meet beautiful women like you."

Celeste waved a hand. "Or maybe this is your house, and you have a wife, or a girlfriend, and you have a kid with her."

"Why would I lie about that?"

"You already lied about whose house this is," she said, raising her voice.

Rolán set the shot glasses down. "I'll show you."

Stepping over to the bookshelf, he found a photo album, and flipped through it, then handed it to Celeste. It was a portrait of a man and a woman and a toddler, the three of them posed and smiling.

"That's my sister," Rolán said, "and that's her husband."

He flipped back a few pages, revealing the same couple. The woman was wearing a wedding dress, and the guy was in a tux.

"My brother-in-law is working in Colorado right now. She went up there with my nephew to visit him."

Celeste flipped through the album. After the wedding shots were photos of them with a baby, and then a toddler. The woman actually did resemble Rolán, around the eyes, and the shape of her face.

"I guess I buy it," she said finally.

"You could be a detective." He took the album and replaced it on the shelf. "Like your friend Truman."

"Lying about stuff takes planning. It's not hard to see that a woman and a kid live here."

Rolán stepped closer, his eyes soft. "It's not really a lie. I just didn't want you to think I was a loser who lives with his parents."

"I live with my parents," Celeste said. "I don't think that defines anyone as a loser."

"It makes it harder to have guests."

"Tell me about it," she said flatly.

Moving closer, Rolán leaned in, and she met his mouth, and grabbed his arms, then felt his chest. He had amazing musculature, lean but taut. She pulled back and took a deep breath. His hands felt so warm.

The tequila shots sat forgotten on the bar cart, and Celeste followed him to the bedroom, glad that he wasn't in a rush. She sat on the bed, and he knelt in front of her, unbuttoning her blouse and exploring her body. By the time he was naked, he was rock hard, and climbed up beside her.

"You need to find a condom," she said, and he did, and she relished the feeling of his skin as he moved closer. His body was a turn-on, and she climaxed before he did.

Afterward, she lay there staring at the ceiling, spaced out, enjoying the feeling of being satiated, and the feeling of Rolán's body next to hers, his arm draped across her belly.

Rolán rolled to the side of the bed, and dug in his jeans, and pulled out his phone. As he lay back again, sinking into the pillows, she watched him unlock it. Not quite able to see the screen, she still recognized the pattern—three digits diagonally from top to bottom, then the last digit back on the same path. She knew the layout of the numbers without even thinking about it. His code had to be 1595.

She felt a little guilty about surreptitiously watching him, noticing that from the corner of her eye. But Truman would call it useful intel. Rolán's face was bathed in the blue glow of the little screen, and she watched him a while longer, then got up and found the bathroom. When she came back, she started to get dressed.

"You can stay for a while, if you want," Rolán said, his brow furrowing.

"I have a thing tomorrow. I need to get some sleep."

He sat up. "Let me drive you home, at least."

"The metro is right over the hill. It's a few minutes' walk."

"I feel like I'm not being a very good host."

Celeste sat with him for a moment and leaned in to kiss him. "You promised fun. I had fun."

———•———

AFTER LUIS HAD GIVEN Beretta a few dollars to keep an eye on his car, he followed Truman upstairs, and they soon wound up in bed. It felt different this time, like things were moving more leisurely. It didn't take much effort for Truman to climax, when Luis was stroking him and their mouths were together.

"That was quick," Luis said, pulling back.

"I couldn't help it. It's because you're so beautiful."

He chuckled. "You definitely know how to lay the mack down."

Truman leaned in, and squeezed his cock, and soon Luis came too. When he shifted onto his back, Luis wrapped an arm across his chest, and soon his breathing lapsed into the regular pattern of sleep. Warm and content and comfortable, Truman looked at the dark sky outside the windows.

This guy and Rolán had grown up in a gang-infested neighborhood. He knew that world was hard to avoid when it was all around. Luis's claim that he'd never been in a gang was believable, he decided. But he wasn't sure if Luis was telling him the whole story about Rolán, or whether the guy was a straight-up hood.

ELEVEN

TRUMAN WOKE IN THE daylight to find Luis sitting on the side of his bed, tying his shoes.

"What time is it?" Truman mumbled.

"Still early. Go back to sleep." He leaned in and kissed him, then stood up and left.

Truman got out of bed anyway, and locked the door, and made espresso. He sat on one of the sofas with his computer and tried to find out more about Rolán. Hernández was such a common surname that there were dozens of different people that appeared in the search results, and he soon gave up.

He was on his second cup of java when his phone buzzed.

"Can you come over here?" Celeste said. "Like,

right now."

"Where are you?"

"At the gallery."

"What's going on? You sound freaked out."

"Just come," she said, and ended the call.

Truman strode over to his clothes rack and got dressed, then hustled down to the street and walked toward the Arts District, assuming his rapid commuter pace.

The neighborhood was busy with delivery vehicles and pedestrians, and Truman dodged handcarts laden with boxes, clothing racks parked outside retail shops, and slow-moving browsers staring in display windows. He breathed deeply and told himself to stay calm. Celeste wasn't easily perturbed, but there had been an edge in her voice.

When he got to the gallery, she was sitting at her desk, and in one of the chairs in front of it was a guy in a dark suit. He turned to look as Truman stepped in. In his forties, maybe, he had a shaved head. It looked good on some black guys, and he was decent looking, lanky and buff. When he rose Truman saw that he was wearing a yellow necktie, and under it was a holster strap that puckered his white shirt. The telltale bulge of a sidearm showed under his suit jacket. He took a deep breath. This guy was a cop.

"Truman, this is Wayne," Celeste said. "Wayne is a G-man."

"Did he drop tin?" Truman said, giving Wayne the once-over.

She frowned. "What?"

"He showed you a badge?"

"I checked his ID. I think it's legit."

Wayne shot her a look. "Of course it's legit."

"I thought you guys traveled in pairs," Truman said.

He shrugged. "Budget cuts."

"What agency are you with?"

"DHS."

Truman frowned. "That's the health department?"

"Homeland Security."

"Of course." Truman nodded. "So have you locked any interesting toddlers in cages recently?"

Wayne pushed the tails of his jacket back, revealing the butt of his sidearm, and put his hands on his hips.

"OK, first," he said, "fuck you. And second, do you really think it's wise to cop an attitude with someone who has the power to arrest you?"

Truman eyed Celeste. "Why is he here? What have you told him?"

"I didn't tell him anything. I thought you might want to hear what he has to say."

He met Wayne's gaze and raised his eyebrows. "Am I being detained?"

Wayne inhaled and held up a palm. "Let's

dial it down a notch. Can we do that? Like I told Ms. De la Torre, I just want to talk."

"Well, have at it."

"Can we sit down, at least?"

Truman pulled the other chair back and turned it to face him, then sat and rested an arm on the edge of Celeste's desk.

"Biff says you can't trust John Law," he said, looking at Celeste. "Some of them are by the book, and some of them are on the take. You never know for sure unless you see him taking a payoff with your own eyes."

Celeste stifled a sigh and looked at Wayne.

"What are you talking about?" Wayne said, his brow furrowing.

"I've got a better one for you," Truman said. "Why are you here?"

"Davit and Mariam Avakian."

"What about them?"

"You have some business dealings with them."

Truman folded his arms. "Might be."

"Wayne knew that I've met with Mariam," Celeste said. "He also knew your name. That's why I called you."

"That has to mean you're tapping their phones, or intercepting their emails. Are they terrorists or something?"

"That's not how this works," Wayne said. "I'm asking the questions."

"And unless you subpoena me, you know I don't have to answer you." Truman threw up his hands. "I'm not saying I won't answer, but you have to give me a reason to."

Wayne clenched his jaw for a moment, then eyed them in turn. "Part of living in a diverse multiethnic country is that all the problems that other places have, all the ethnic and religious conflicts, tend to show up here too."

"You can skip ahead a little," Celeste said, waving a hand. "We know what kind of country we live in."

Wayne shot her a look. "Davit Avakian has been linked to an overseas group that provides arms to the Armenians."

"Are they a terrorist group?" she said.

"Not technically."

"So why are you surveilling him?"

"Global politics is complicated. We can't have Americans conducting their own foreign policy. It's illegal."

"I'm no political scientist," Celeste said, "but my understanding is that the Turks have been trying to trample the Armenians for centuries. Turkey is our NATO ally, so technically that makes the Armenians our enemy."

"That doesn't follow. International relations are more complex."

Celeste gestured languorously. "Like I said,

I'm just a tyro with this stuff."

"Maybe I can simplify things," Truman said. "I don't know anything about Davo's and Mariam's politics, or their connections overseas."

"Ditto," Celeste said. "I'm helping Mariam acquire artworks for her decorating clients. We're sourcing them right here in LA. It's strictly business."

"And you?" Wayne said, eyeing Truman. "What's your connection?"

He took a deep breath. If he lied to this guy, he'd be in for a world of pain. Cops always knew when you were lying, and even if they didn't, they had massive resources to check—huge office buildings full of people with nothing but time to follow up and verify or disprove anything that he said.

"Is it still a crime to lie to a federal agent?"

Wayne nodded. "Totally."

"See, you could be lying about that, and I'd have no way of knowing."

"Is Homeland Security even a legit law-enforcement agency?" Celeste said. "There are so damn many of them. Dozens of little government offices that nobody's ever heard of. The federal mint employees tennis-shoe police, and the national monument firewood inspection agency."

Wayne ignored her and eyed Truman. "Why would you want to lie to me?" he demanded. "It tells me that you're up to something."

"I'm not," Truman said, and raised his eyebrows. "Here's the deal. A client of mine has a personal beef with Davo. It's a former employee, and the dispute is over property. He hired me to look into it."

"Who is this person?"

"That's confidential."

Wayne scoffed. "A client for what, exactly?"

"I do investigations," Truman said.

His eyes narrowed. "You're a PI?"

"I'm not licensed. I just do research to help people."

"And you have a permit to carry a firearm?"

Truman waved a hand. "I don't know anything about guns."

"You can't do that," Wayne said, staring at him.

"What, do research? Help people? What law am I breaking?"

"You can't go around posing as a detective."

"I never said I was a PI, or a security guard, or a cop, or whatever it is that you are." Truman held up his palm and swirled it at him. "What I do is different. It involves finesse and reasoning. Not the brute-force stuff."

"You're going to get yourself shot."

"Well, I appreciate your concern."

Wayne sat back in his chair. "Is your client one of the warehouse guys?"

"Are Davo's staff involved in this Armenian armaments business?" Truman said.

"He's not going to tell you one way or the other," Celeste said. "That's the thing about law enforcement. Information goes in, absolutely nothing comes out."

Wayne eyed her. "None of Davit's employees are under investigation." Looking at Truman, he said, "So you're not involved with his business."

"I've never even met the guy," Truman said. "Are you actively investigating the Avakians? Like in your office, with a team of people dressed in bland clothes, and driver's license photos blown up and taped to a whiteboard? Or are you poking around on your own, just in case you can rattle something loose?"

Rising from his chair, Wayne buttoned his jacket. "Thanks for your time today."

"Is part of coming here to intimidate us into not working with the Avakians?" Celeste said.

Truman stood up too. "I'm not sure I like Uncle Sam telling me who I can associate with."

"He's not," Wayne said, his tone sharp. "And I'm not." He looked from him to Celeste. "You two are something else."

"You didn't get my phone number," Truman said. He dug in his hip pocket, and produced a dog-eared business card, and handed it to Wayne.

"Thanks," he said flatly, and tucked it away

without glancing at it.

"You really should call him," Celeste said. "Truman has a thing for cops."

"No, I don't." He turned to Wayne. "But maybe I should get your number too."

"It's not going to work," he said. "Cops and robbers don't mix."

"I'm not a crook, you arrogant stuffed shirt."

"But you are a witness."

"To nothing," Truman said, raising his voice. "Maybe a better label is victim of federal harassment."

"You actually want me to go out with you, even though you're yelling at me right now?"

"Just call me when you've cooled down. We'll go for a drink or something. Nothing heavy."

"I'm not the one who needs to cool down," he shouted.

Truman raised his eyebrows. "If you say so."

Wayne scoffed and moved toward the door, slamming it behind him as he left.

"I can't believe you hit on that guy," Celeste said. "I just thought you should meet him. So did he."

"You sounded weird on the phone." Truman dropped into his chair again.

"I was a little rattled when he first showed up. They do that thing, right, the bully persona, the tough talk, flashing the badge. I guess I was a little freaked out that some federal agency had taken an interest in you and me personally. You didn't have to tell him what you were up to, though."

"I didn't tell him all that because I felt intimidated. I don't even think that was his main purpose. He came alone, right, so he's just pulling on stray threads. I figured unless I told him the broad strokes, he would have kept pressing me, or pressing us, until it made sense to him. And we're not involved in Davo's politics. A stripped-down version of the truth seemed like the easiest way."

She pursed her lips. "That actually does sound expedient. Let's hope it works. With luck, Wayne will back off."

"The feds have to be monitoring their phone calls," Truman said. "We've both called Mariam, and I've called Davo. Wayne did mention both their names."

"Wayne knows who they're talking to, but maybe he doesn't know what they're saying. If he did, it wouldn't require a visit. Maybe it's like you said—Wayne is just pulling at loose threads."

"I know it's a lot easier to get call metadata than it is to actually wiretap someone." Truman waved a hand. "Him showing up here, though, makes me think Davo might be a little dangerous."

"So what if the feds don't like his politics?"

Celeste said. "It doesn't mean anything. They keep tabs on lots of people. Those idiots gang-stalked John Lennon because he used the word 'peace,' and then that movie actress whose only crime was dating a black guy."

"Wayne did say Davo isn't a terrorist."

"Indirectly. But yeah, he did say that."

Truman took a breath and ran a hand through his hair. "So I saw Luis last night. He talked about Rolán. According to him neither of them were in a gang, but they weren't far from that world."

"I saw Rolán last night," Celeste said. "He's not a thug."

His eyes narrowed. "You slept with him. It took you long enough."

Celeste laughed. "I'm not sex-first like you are."

"It got me to thinking. I'm starting to wonder if Rolán is lying about the hit-and-run and the helmet."

"Why would he do that?"

"It feels like he's less concerned about the actual helmet than he is with breaking into Davo's house," Truman said. "He doesn't want me to tell Davo that I know him."

"I can understand that. It would turn up the heat."

"I'm going to meet Davo today. Maybe I'll get a better sense of who he is."

"Local blackmailer and international scoff-law," Celeste said, "or perhaps something else."

"There you go."

"So is Luis a hood?"

"He has a job," Truman said, "and he goes to college. He shares a lot of information with Rolán. It's hard to say."

"I guess it's hard to be objective about him when you're sleeping with him."

"Guilty." Truman threw up his hands. "When is your design event with Mariam?"

"Soon," Celeste said. "I should probably go."

"Does Saffron know you're moonlighting?"

"She's fine with it. As long as the gallery gets a cut of any artist that we're repping."

A noise came from the back of the gallery— the fire door opened and then slammed shut.

"The woman herself," Celeste said.

Saffron strode in, her black hair perfectly coiffed, tumbling to her shoulders. The suit she was wearing was a deep-yellow shade that made her dark skin glow. With huge lapels, it looked like a zoot suit, but it must be in style. If Saffron was wearing it, Celeste knew, it was likely couture.

"Truman, dear," she said, stopping in front of them. "I love what you've done with your hair."

"Thanks," he said, and self-consciously ran a hand through it. "That's a great suit."

Saffron arched her eyebrows. "I know."

"I have an event today," Celeste said, "but if you're here, I won't lock up."

"Something fun?"

"It's a seminar on women in design."

"Oh—I wanted to go to that." Saffron made pouty lips.

"So come with me. We'll lock up the gallery."

"I'm not dressed for it. I'm working a different look here."

"You look fine," Celeste said, and gestured to her suit. "You'll look better than anyone else in the room."

Saffron hesitated, but then said, "OK. But let me fix my makeup."

"You just got in."

"I won't be a minute. You'll have to drive."

"Didn't you drive here?"

"Of course, sweetie, but if it's a seminar, I'll be drinking."

Saffron walked around under the stairs, where the restroom was.

"Is it wise to introduce her to Mariam?" Truman said quietly. "She might poach the work you're doing with her."

Celeste shook her head. "Saffron would never take that kind of work. There's not enough profit or prestige. Mariam might have a few clients with big budgets, but mostly it'll be low-budget kitsch stuff and emerging artists."

"I get it. Biff says skip the penny-ante jobs unless you're hungry."

"I'm hungry," she said, and rose. "Saffron isn't."

TWELVE

TRUMAN WALKED TO A coffeehouse near the gallery, and bought a bagel, and sat in the window to eat it. He'd left his place in such a rush that he'd neglected to bring his backpack, with his computer and his notebooks, and now he didn't have time to go back for it. On his phone he checked the address of Davo's warehouse. It was in Vernon, not too far away, and surprisingly close to a metro station.

After he'd eaten, he headed to the train, and was soon walking through the industrial neighborhood between the rail line and Davo's place. The streets were wide, built for semi-trailer traffic, and among the sprawling low-slung warehouses there seemed to be a lot of food suppliers. The smell that hung in the air was cloyingly sweet and sulfuric, like rotting produce.

Davo's warehouse was hard to miss, with big blue letters on the wall that spelled out AVAKIAN. There were a couple of truck docks on the side of the structure, but right now the loading bay doors were rolled closed. A tan-colored shipping container sat on a flatbed trailer in the yard next to them.

Parked near the front, adjacent to the office door, were several vehicles, one of them the familiar dark-green Bimmer.

Truman pushed open the pedestrian door and found himself in a spartan front office. Mariam clearly hadn't been asked to decorate in here. Two desks sat on a threadbare gray carpet, with the office's lone occupant seated at one of them. She was in her fifties, with dark hair, and wore a simple white blouse. As Truman stepped in, she looked up at him.

"Can I help you?"

"I'm here to see Davo," he said.

Before she could reply, Davo appeared from one of the doorways behind her.

"Mr. Truman," he said, his voice booming. He stepped toward him, and reached for his hand, and gave it a powerful squeeze.

"It's just Truman."

"I thought it was your family name."

"That's Boudreaux," he said. "Truman Boudreaux."

"Do you have a business card?"

He patted his pants pocket and frowned. "I don't. I can write it down if you'd like." No way could he give this guy his card—it would blow his cover, as it had the word *investigations* printed under his name.

"Don't bother. I have your phone number. Why are English names so difficult?"

"Technically it's a French name. By way of Massachusetts."

"We'll go into my office," Davo said. "Do you want a coffee? I'll warn you, though: I make it the Eastern way."

"Greek-style? I love Greek coffee."

He turned to the woman at the desk. "Could you make us a pot?"

"Of course," she said, and got up.

Davo waved for Truman to follow, and led him through a doorway into another office. This one felt utilitarian, like the front office, but filling one wall was a window that looked onto a yawning warehouse space. The only activity inside right now was a guy driving a little yellow forklift. It looked like he was stacking empty pallets.

Next to the glass was a strange desk that looked like the slab on top might be too heavy for the rattan base. At one side of the room was a set of narrow blue club chairs, and on the wall above them hung an image of a big bird with its wings outspread. An eagle, maybe. It wasn't a painting, but some kind of sculpture, made of little pieces of crumpled reflective foil. So shiny and lurid, it was hard to pull his eyes away.

"Have a seat," Davo said, waving to the club chairs, and eased into one himself. It looked too small for him.

"So why do you say it's Greek?" Davo said, his brow furrowing. "Most people call it Turkish coffee."

"I've never been to Turkey, but I've been to Greece. I love it there. The people, and the islands, and especially the coffee."

Davo sat back, a wry smile on his face. "Oh, Truman—you and I are going to get along just fine."

"So what do you do here?" He gestured to the window into the warehouse.

"I import furniture and artworks. My desk, for example, and this." He gestured to the shiny bird on the wall.

"That's quite the eagle."

"Thank you."

"How many employees do you have?"

"You met Lina in the front office, and there's three or four guys who work in the warehouse. They unpack the shipping containers, and move the furniture, and deliver it to my customers."

"That means retail shops?" Truman said.

"Mostly."

Lina stepped in, carrying a tray with a pot and two little cups, and set it on the low table between them.

Davo thanked her, and added, "Close the door on your way out." To Truman, he said, "Enjoy."

It was strong and sweet, he found, sipping at the black liquid.

"This stuff is totally addictive."

"Let me explain my problem," Davo said, cradling his little cup in his meaty hands. "I need to ship something abroad. It needs to be packed so that it's not obvious what it is. Concealed in some way."

"In my business we call that smuggling."

He scowled and waved dismissively. "It's nothing illegal. But it's valuable, and I don't want the middlemen to steal from me."

"What kind of thing are you shipping abroad?"

"I can't really tell you that."

"OK." Truman watched him for a moment. "How big is it, then, and how heavy, and how fragile?"

"Like this," he said, holding his hands in the air, about a foot apart. "We can configure the shape. It's quite heavy, like metal, but it's not fragile."

The phone on his desk rang, and Davo glanced at his chunky gold wristwatch, then sat up and set down his coffee.

"I apologize," he said, "but I have to take this call."

"I'll step outside." Truman sat up.

"Don't bother." Davo waved for him to stay and hustled over to his desk.

As he sat back again, Davo dropped into his desk chair, and picked up the call, and spoke in Armenian. Truman pulled out his phone and started his audio recorder, then stared at the screen as if he were reading. Davo's tone grew more emphatic, even angry. He was talking more than he was listening. If Truman hadn't known what language it was, he would never be able to identify it. The rhythm and the sharp consonants sounded vaguely Middle Eastern.

When Davo hung up the receiver, Truman killed the recorder and tucked his phone away, then drained his little cup to the dregs, waiting for Davo to return.

"So what do you think?" Davo said, as he sat across from him.

"I wish you could show me exactly what it is that you're talking about."

"In general terms, then." He spread his palms. "How would you handle it as a shipping challenge?"

"I have to say it's not something I've come across before. The idea of disguising something valuable, I mean. I could tell you about packing materials and padding, but not much about stealth. Can you give me a day or two to think about it?"

"Of course."

Davo drained his cup, then rose, and walked Truman out to the front office.

"Thanks for the coffee," Truman said to Lina as he passed her desk. He stepped out the front door, surprised that Davo followed him.

"I'm thinking the Bimmer is yours," Truman said, gesturing to the vehicles.

"Why do you say that?"

"You don't seem like the kind of guy who'd go around in a ten-year-old Corolla, or a rusty pickup."

Davo threw his head back and guffawed.

"I don't see that model very often," Truman said. In reality he didn't pay much attention to cars, but Rolán had told him this vehicle was unique.

"I had to go to Arizona to buy it," Davo said. "The engine is too big for California."

"You don't commute by motorcycle? You could split the lanes, and zip through all the traffic on the 101."

"I'm not a teenager," Davo said, and frowned.

"I don't have a motorcycle. Do you know what happens to guys my age who have a midlife crisis and start riding those things? If they're lucky, they get a wheelchair, because they suddenly have no legs. If they're not so lucky, they wind up in a wooden box six feet down."

"Neither one sounds like an optimal outcome," Truman said. "Anyway, I'll be in touch."

"Where's your car? I came out to see what you're driving."

"I took the metro."

Davo's face fell. "I'm so sorry. Do you want me to call you a cab?"

"I actually like taking the metro," he said, and clapped Davo on the shoulder before he turned and walked toward the street.

———◆———

ONCE HE WAS HOME, Truman settled in at his desk and listened to the recording he'd made. There was a bit of an echo, as he'd taped it from across the room, but Davo's voice was clear. He sent Celeste a text:

> Let me know when you're done with your event.
> We can get a coffee and debrief.

It was hours later when Truman got a reply:

> Leaving here soon. Meet you at that coffeehouse across from the square.

He locked up his loft and set off walking. Davo's Greek coffee must have been strong, as he still felt a little wired, and the caffeine put a spring in his step. When he got to the place, he ordered a soda water and sat near the window.

When Celeste walked in, she waved and went to the counter, and came over a minute later with a little cup of espresso, dropping into the chair across from him.

"How was the event?" Truman said. "Did Saffron and Mariam get along?"

"They just met briefly," Celeste said, and sipped from her cup. "We all went to different seminars. Mariam was right—it expanded my understanding of the design business in this town."

"Ooh, look at you, working the network."

She chuckled at that. "How was your meeting with Davo?"

Truman explained what Davo had asked him. "Basically he wants me to help him smuggle something out of the country."

"It has to be related to what G-man Wayne was talking about, don't you think?"

"That seems likely."

"If he's worried about it getting intercepted, it's probably something negotiable, like cash."

"He said it was heavy, like metal."

"Guns and ammunition, maybe?" Celeste said. "You wouldn't want that intercepted either."

"So Davo took a call while I was sitting there. I couldn't understand what he was saying, but he sounded kind of angry. I recorded it."

"If he did it in front of you, it probably wasn't anything secret."

"I bet he just thought I wouldn't understand," Truman said. "He was speaking Armenian. We should get it translated."

"You mean another trip to see Sosi."

"Unless you've been learning Armenian."

She dug out her phone and dialed. "Hey, girl. Are you at work?" A minute later she ended the call. "*Vámonos,*" she said to Truman. "Sosi said we can drop by her shop."

He took another swig of soda water and then followed her out to the street.

"Let's walk," Celeste said. "It's only a few blocks."

"We should take her a gift."

"You want to stop and get her a corsage?"

"Not that, but something," Truman said. "We've been bugging her a lot."

"It has to be something consumable."

"Booze, maybe? Candy?"

"I remember one time she and I went to a deli in the Jewelry District. She practically had an orgasm over this moussaka and black olive sandwich."

"So let's get her one," Truman said. "It's almost

on the way."

They walked down to Seventh Street, and into an alley, where Celeste pointed out the deli. She went to the counter and ordered the sandwich.

Truman lingered in the alley out front, and pulled out his phone, and dialed Rolán's number. His voice mail answered.

"I met with Davo," Truman told the machine. "You'll be happy to hear that nobody mentioned you. But I did ask him about riding. He denies that he even has a motorcycle. Maybe you could clarify."

He ended the call and stepped into the deli.

"Is that everything?" the clerk said, tucking the sandwich into a bag.

"Give me a black-and-white cookie," Truman said, eyeing it in the display case.

"For Sosi?" Celeste said.

"For me. I'm going to eat it on the way."

"Two black-and-whites," Celeste said, and then paid for everything.

They munched on their cookies as they walked up Seventh Street, the sandwich dangling from Celeste's other hand. She wiped her fingers on one of the napkins the clerk had thrown in the bag.

"That was pretty good," she said.

"A little dry." Truman's mouth was still half full. "And not as sweet as it could be."

"You did manage to scarf down the whole thing, though, despite its flaws."

Truman laughed, and had to cover his mouth. That made her laugh too. She loved that about him, the glaring lack of self-awareness that he sometimes displayed.

When they stepped into the print shop, Sosi was ringing up a customer, and they waited for her as the guy thanked her and then turned to leave.

"Look at you two," Sosi said. "I just saw you on Saturday."

"A small gift," Celeste said, and set the sandwich on the counter.

She opened the bag and sniffed. "Is this what I think it is?"

"That depends on what you think it is."

"Moussaka and black olives, sent directly from heaven."

"You're exactly right," Celeste said.

"How did you know I'd be hangry right about now?"

"It was Truman's idea, although I'm the one who thought of that specific sandwich."

"Can I show you that writing again?" Truman said. "Just to confirm my understanding." He dug out his phone, and found the photo of the hand-writing on the envelope, and handed it to Sosi.

"The Armenian part says 'twenty-three.' It's

written clearly. The meaning is unambiguous."

"Great—that's what I remembered."

"There's one other thing," Celeste said. "A recording in Armenian. Could you translate?"

Sosi waved a hand. "I can try."

Setting his phone on the countertop, Truman played the clip of Davo through the little speaker. Sosi's brow furrowed as she listened intently. When it ended, she met his gaze.

"Someone's been spying."

He could feel his face heating up. "What were they talking about?"

"I can only hear one side of the conversation."

"He was on the phone," Truman said.

She held his gaze. "Who is this guy?"

"Well, he's Armenian."

"I know that much," Sosi said, and sighed. "He says, 'I'll get them out of the country,' and 'It's going to take a short time.' He also uses a phrase that means something like 'ready to go.' After that he's just reassuring the other person that he's not messing around, that he's sincere. He says it three different ways. The last thing he says is 'The payment is coming to you.'"

"'I'll get them out of the country,'" Celeste said. "Is there any indication of what he's talking about?"

"Something plural," Sosi said. "That's all I got."

"That's really helpful," Truman said.

"So you're not going to tell me anything about him? I might know the guy, or my uncles might."

"That's why I can't tell you. It's confidential."

Sosi nodded. "Thanks for the sandwich."

When they got out to the street, Celeste said, "Do you think that bar is open? The one with all the books. It's right near here."

"I love that place," Truman said. "If I were running a bar in the Financial District, I'd definitely be open right now. It's almost quitting time for all these office drones."

It was open, they found, when they walked around the corner. The place looked like a library, with shelves of books lining the walls. It was small, with just a few tables and barstools, and they sat at the bar.

The bartender had short platinum-blond hair with black roots, and she flashed Celeste a smile when she stepped over.

"A gin and tonic," Celeste said, "and a blended margarita for my friend."

"Do you care what kind of gin?"

"Whatever's in the well."

She nodded and stepped away, and Celeste eyed Truman. He sat with his arms folded, staring absently at the shelves of bottles, a grim look on his face. He looked at Celeste when he noticed her gaze.

"Everybody's playing me," he said.

"What are you talking about?"

"Davo wants me to help him smuggle something out of the country. A payment, Sosi said. If it's not weapons, it's probably funding for weapons, like Wayne said. And Rolán lied to me too."

"This morning you weren't sure about Rolán."

"Davo doesn't have a motorcycle. He doesn't even ride. That means Rolán's story is bogus."

"Or Davo is the one who's lying," Celeste said.

"Why would he lie about that? He doesn't know I'm connected to Rolán. Think about it. Rolán said Davo borrowed a helmet for his wife. Can you imagine Davo and Mariam riding around on a motorcycle?"

Celeste bit her lip. "That does sound far-fetched. They seem more like indoor people."

The bartender set down their drinks, and Truman pulled out his wad of cash to pay for them.

Once they'd clinked glasses, Celeste said, "I was thinking about the numbers you showed Sosi. Show me that envelope again."

Truman dug out his phone and pulled up the photo.

"We decided it meant Hollywood Storage," she said.

"You think it means something else?"

"I think we got it right, but the 'Hollywood' could have a different meaning. What if it's not the name of the business, but it means it's in that neighborhood?"

Truman set down his tumbler. "So it means a self-storage place somewhere in actual Hollywood, not out in NoHo?"

"It definitely wasn't the one we broke into."

He tapped a finger to his lips. "We didn't break in. We sort of had a key."

"Emphasis on 'sort of.'"

"Those self-storage places are everywhere. There are probably dozens of them in Hollywood. I wouldn't know where to start."

"I was thinking about that too," Celeste said. "Yesterday Davo left for a while. He said he had an errand. Mariam was hassling him about it. He said it wouldn't take long because it was right off the freeway."

Truman sat up. "Knowing where his warehouse is, logically he takes the Hollywood Freeway to get to work every day."

"I'm sure that's what he meant."

"So maybe it's a storage place that's right off that freeway."

"There can't be many that fit that configuration," Celeste said.

"Right on." He cracked a smile, and held up a palm, and Celeste slapped it. "I'm so glad you thought of that. You're a genius."

"It's nice to have that immutable fact

acknowledged once in a while," she said, swirling the ice in her highball, "but let's see if we can actually find it."

Truman looked at his phone and scoured the map. "There's three of them that might fit," he said finally, and showed her the screen.

"The one at the top is close to the freeway, but it's not near an exit," she said, taking the phone. "The other two are."

She tapped on the listing, and then the second one, as Truman leaned in to look.

"I've never seen that place," he said, "but I know about the other one. It's in a prewar heritage building."

"What was it before it was self-storage?"

"It was built as a warehouse, so it's always been for storage. It's unusual because on the outside it's a glam high-rise."

"Should we go have a look?" Celeste said.

"The high-rise, or the other one?"

"The other one is closer to Davo's house."

Truman lifted his glass. "Are we too loaded?"

"We'll burn it off. We have to walk back to my car, and presumably we'll have to swing by your place to get your 'keys.'" She waggled her fingers to put air quotes around the word.

"Let's go," he said, and slammed the last of his margarita.

THIRTEEN

O N THE WALK TO the car, Truman could feel the booze, but the buzz had faded by the time they pulled up at his loft. He ran up the stairs and went in just long enough to grab his lock-picking kit, then hustled back down.

Celeste got on the freeway, and merged onto the 101 as the last of the daylight was fading in the west. The storage place was just a block from the exit. She parked farther up the street at a meter, and they walked back.

The building came right to the sidewalk, and in the twilight it looked to have just one level. The steel shutter was rolled down on the vehicle entrance. Next to it the pedestrian entrance was a glass door into a brightly lit office, where a guy sat behind the counter, staring at a computer.

"Fancy place," Celeste said, pausing on the sidewalk and eyeing the purple neon sign overhead. "How do we get in?"

"I have an idea," Truman said, and stepped into the office.

The clerk was a gray-haired guy, with leathery skin and bushy black eyebrows, and he looked up as they walked in.

"Do you have any units available?" Truman said.

"Sure," the guy said, straightening up. He had a trace of an accent, maybe Russian. "Five-by-seven is two hundred a month, and ten-by-ten is four hundred."

"Whoa," Celeste said. "I had no idea they cost that much."

The guy frowned. "All the units are climate-controlled, and very secure."

"Still," she said. "This is East Hollywood, not a Bel Air ridgetop with a view."

"I have many high-end clients," he said, raising his voice. "I don't rent to just anyone."

Truman held up a hand. "Can I look at one?"

"There's only the two sizes available. What do you need to store?"

"If I could go inside the unit, I'd get the sense of whether it would work."

"Fine. Check out 104 and 123. They aren't

locked." As they moved toward the inner doorway, he said, "No monkey business. I'll look for you back here in ten minutes."

Truman frowned at that but didn't respond.

The door led into a broad hallway. It was wide enough for a vehicle, with the steel-shutter door at the end, and overhead there was no ceiling, just open sky.

"He's not very trusting," Celeste said, once they were out of earshot.

"I'm shocked that he thought we looked like we were up to something."

"We are up to something."

"Still," Truman said.

"I see a problem—look at the numbers. 105, 107. Three digits. Maybe this isn't the place."

He sighed. "Or we're just wrong about everything."

"Let's make sure," she said, and they walked to the end of the aisle, then down the next one.

"Here's unit 123." Truman stopped in front of the shutter. "Every number starts with a 1. I wonder if Davo wrote 23 to mean 123?"

"That's one of the ones the clerk said to look inside. There's no padlock on it, see?"

Truman rolled the door partway up, and flicked on the light, revealing an empty space with a bare concrete floor.

"I'm thinking this is completely the wrong

place," Celeste said, watching him pull the door down again. "But let's walk to the end."

Eventually satisfied there was no unit 23, they walked back to the office.

"What did you think?" the clerk said, looking up from his screen as they came in.

"It's not going to work," Celeste said.

"You need a bigger one? I might have something opening up next week. After the forfeiture auction."

"It's not that. It's just that there's a weird smell."

"What are you talking about?" he demanded. "In which unit?"

She wrinkled her nose. "It's kind of everywhere."

"Nothing smells in here," he said, raising his voice.

"It's just too down-market for us," Truman said. "But thanks anyway."

"I'll show you down-market," he shouted.

Celeste was already at the door to the street, and Truman hustled out after her.

"You piece of trash," the guy shouted after them. "Get out of my store."

Walking back to the car, they both laughed, and Truman glanced over his shoulder to make sure the guy wasn't following them.

"That was mean," he said.

"He's the one with class issues. I didn't install his buttons. It was easy enough to press them, though."

"Let's try the other place," he said, as they climbed into her car.

Celeste drove down Vermont, then east again toward the freeway. Truman pointed out the tower, looming over the street ahead, its stature unique in the neighborhood.

"It's kind of glam," she said. "I must have driven by it a thousand times, but I never looked closely."

They parked a half block past it and walked back. The vehicle driveway was dark, with the barred gate across it closed. The pedestrian entrance was a tall steel gate with a lighted numeric keypad at the side.

"There's no lock to pick," Celeste said.

Truman surveyed the gate, and looked through the metal bars. "I think someone's coming."

He moved to the keypad and took out his wallet, then pulled it open, digging through its contents as if he were looking for something. A guy pushed on the crash bar and stepped through the gate. As it swung open, Truman ignored him, focused instead on his task. Celeste grabbed the gate before it swung closed. The guy didn't look back.

"Nicely done," Truman said quietly. He tucked

his wallet away and followed her inside.

"There are lots of cameras here," she said, as they strode over to the high-rise and into the lobby.

"We're not doing anything wrong. No one's going to check the video."

When he pressed the call button, the door slowly rolled open to reveal a big freight elevator. Inside, the unit numbers were listed next to the floor buttons, and Truman pressed the one marked 20 TO 39.

The elevator lumbered slowly upward, and they stepped off into a wide hallway. No one else was around, and they walked until they found unit 23.

"Are we on camera here?" Truman said, under his breath.

"There's just one. At the far end of the hall." Celeste stepped to the side of the unit's roll-up door, casually resting her hand on the wall. "You're out of its view now."

"This padlock matches the key in Davo's envelope. It's the same as the one I bought to practice on."

"That seems like a good sign."

Truman pulled his lock-picking kit out of his hip pocket, and zipped it open, and knelt in front of the lock. Celeste watched him work, manipulating the little tools with both hands.

"The trick is to depress the right tumblers and get it rotating at the same time," he said.

"No pressure, but the sooner you get it open, the better."

A moment later she heard the lock pop open.

"Yeah, baby," Truman said. "Smooth like the rumba."

Celeste wanted to say *You're dancing your way into a felony*, but she held her tongue, and rolled up the door once Truman had pulled the lock off. She found the light switch and flicked it on, and once they were both inside, pulled the door down.

"This is more like it," Truman said. "It's the same kind of stuff Davo has in his office at the warehouse."

Rattan lounge chairs, Celeste saw, and a headboard for a bed leaning against the wall, made of dark wood with a carved bas-relief design. Bedside tables were stacked on end tables, and a gray love seat sat against the back wall.

"Again," she said, "if he has a whole warehouse for this stuff, why would he put it here?"

"Maybe to hide other stuff."

Truman pulled open the drawers on the bedside tables, then leaned over them to look behind them. Celeste stepped over and looked behind the love seat, surprised at how easy it was to pull out from the wall.

"This stuff is so light," she said.

"It's basically made of straw."

"There's no helmet here," she said finally. "There's nowhere that we haven't looked that's big enough to stash one."

Truman went to look behind the headboard, pulling it away from the wall.

"Hold up," Celeste said, and he turned to look. She'd pulled open the bottom drawer of a tall dresser next to the little sofa. Inside were two bags made of heavy black canvas. "Do those look familiar?"

It was the same kind of bag they kept their cash in, stashed in the wall in Truman's loft.

"So what's inside?" he said.

"Should we be wearing gloves?"

"We're not going to take anything. It won't matter."

"So I'm the one who's supposed to open them?"

Truman flapped his hand. "You found them."

She huffed as she knelt and pulled on the heavy zipper of one of the bags, revealing the contents. It was full of gleaming gold coins. She sat back and stared at them.

"Whoa." Truman stooped to pick up one of the coins, then held it in the light to examine it. One side bore the image of a buffalo, and on the reverse was the profile of an elderly man with feathers in his hair. "This is a legit coin. It says 'United States' on it."

"They look like gold," Celeste said. "Don't you think that's what it is? If it's real, there's an awful lot of it."

"Look at the way it shines. Nothing but gold looks like that."

"Do you think they're antiques? From the gold rush days?"

"This one is dated 2012."

She pulled the bag open wider. "Look at how many there are."

"I'd call that a fuck-ton."

Celeste pulled the zipper to open the other bag. "Same thing." She dug into them with a finger. "I think they're all the same kind of coin, with the buffalo and the old guy."

He knelt beside her and tossed the coin back in the bag. They spent a quiet moment, both of them gazing at the intensity of the hoard.

"It has gravity, doesn't it?" Truman said. "It's different than folding money."

"I feel it too. It's almost hypnotic."

"I wonder what all this is worth."

"I'm sure we can find out the value of each coin," Celeste said, "but do you really want to count them?"

"We don't have to. I saw a luggage scale."

"Is that like a bathroom scale?"

Truman rose and stepped across the space. "It's portable, so you can use it at the airport. You hang your suitcase on it to see what it weighs."

He found the device, and reached up to hang it on one of the I-beams that ran across the ceiling.

"I get it," Celeste said, and zipped the bags closed. She lifted one out, using both hands. The coins shifted and rattled dully as she moved the bag. "This is freaking heavy."

Carrying it over to Truman, she looped the handle over the hook at the bottom of the scale.

"Just about forty pounds," Truman said, peering at the readout.

Celeste lifted the bag off, and put it in the drawer again, shaking it to redistribute the coins, then carried the other one over to the scale.

"This one is thirty-five."

"So Davo has seventy-five pounds of gold coins. It has to be worth a fortune."

She lifted the bag off and set it in the drawer again, kneeling to adjust them so that they looked the way they had when she'd found them.

"This has to be what he wants to smuggle," Truman said. "It's as good as cash, and anyone who intercepted it could just steal it."

Celeste slid the drawer closed and stood up, slapping the dust off her knees. "Let's get out of here."

Once he'd put the luggage scale back where he'd found it, Truman followed her out, and pulled the door down, and snapped on the padlock.

They were both quiet as they walked to the elevator and rode down to the lobby. Once they were through the gate and on the street, Celeste spoke.

"That's so not a secure hiding place. We walked right in."

"I was wondering about that," Truman said. "It makes me think that no one but Davo knows the stash is there. Remember what he said in that phone call he made? I bet it's not going to be there for long."

"We probably could have taxed a few coins. I doubt Davo would have noticed."

Truman scoffed. "That's not who we are."

"I forgot," Celeste said. "We only steal from drug dealers."

"That cash was destined for a police evidence locker. It's not the same."

"Do you want to eat?" Celeste said, stepping around her car and climbing in behind the wheel. "That place in the old theater is almost on the way downtown."

Truman assented, and soon they had a table in the corner, in the cavernous brick space where the movie screen used to be. Celeste ordered a salad, and Truman ordered a little pizza, and they both asked for draft beer.

"Those coins are called the buffalo medallion,"

Truman said, gazing at his phone. "It's a re-creation of an old nickel. Each of them is exactly one ounce of gold."

Celeste did the calculation. "Seventy-five pounds, one ounce per coin. That means there's about twelve hundred coins. What are they worth?"

"This says it's not like circulating money. The government mints them, but the coin's value isn't set. It's worth what the metal is worth, so it fluctuates with the price of gold. Today you could sell one for about two grand."

"That much?" Celeste raised her eyebrows, then worked through the numbers in her head. "That means Davo has two and a half million bucks' worth of gold secured with a padlock." She shook her head in disbelief. "I hope nobody else knows about it."

Their drinks arrived, and Truman tapped her glass with his. "Here's to discretion."

FOURTEEN

AFTER THEY'D EATEN, WALKING abreast on the way to the car, Truman's phone buzzed. It was a 213 number, which meant it was local, but it didn't have a name associated with it. He picked up anyway and said, "Boudreaux."

"It's Wayne," he said. "You and I met earlier today."

"I remember."

"I was wondering about that drink. I'm leaving my office soon. I could meet you between here and your place."

"Where's your office?" Truman said.

"In the federal building."

"Which federal building? Those are all over the place."

"Downtown. In the Civic Center."

"Wait—you know where I live?"

"It's on your business card," Wayne said.

"No, it's not."

Celeste stepped around to the driver's side of her little car, and Truman climbed in the passenger seat.

"I might have looked it up," Wayne said.

"Such a snoop."

"Don't get upset. How about that drink?"

"Do you know the place that's around the corner from the police station? The one that's in a basement."

Once he'd ended the call, Celeste said, "You're meeting Wayne."

"Just for a drink."

She clicked on her headlights and nosed the vehicle into the street. "You're going to climb that man like a tree."

Truman laughed. "We'll see what happens."

"Are you going to tell him about Davo's stash?"

"No freaking way. It's none of his business, and it's none of Uncle Sam's business. It's not illegal to have money."

"That sounds right," Celeste said, braking for a red light. "You know he's just meeting you to pump you for more information, though, right? He'll try to get a couple drinks into you so that you'll let your guard down."

"I think I can handle that. Biff says don't confide anything to anyone unless it's something you don't mind seeing in the newspaper."

"Just don't overdrink."

"Thank you for the guidance," Truman said flatly. "Could you drop me on Second Street?"

———◆———

WAYNE WAS ALREADY AT the bar when he walked in, parked on a stool and facing the room, his elbows resting on the bar top behind him. He was still wearing a suit, but he'd loosened his tie, and Truman could see the contours of his well-defined pecs. This guy really was hot. When he caught sight of Truman, he jutted his chin and smiled. Truman took the stool beside him and signaled the bartender.

When the guy stepped over, he said, "A blended margarita."

"I like this place," Wayne said. "I've never been down here."

"It was a generating station back in the day." Truman swiveled around to face the room and gestured to the row of antique turbines that ran its length. "The electricity grid didn't really start to expand until the 1940s. This kind of technology quickly became obsolete. They sat here unused for decades."

"Until someone had the vision to do this."

"I'm thinking it was cheaper to build a bar around it than to haul it out as scrap metal."

"You know a lot about the place," Wayne said. "You could give tours."

Truman's drink arrived, and once he'd paid for it, he tapped it against Wayne's beer glass and took a sip.

"I actually used to be a tour guide."

"That seems like a more appropriate job for you than what you're doing now."

Truman scowled. "I already have a mother," he said, raising his voice. "I don't need your input about what I should be doing for work."

"Relax. I'm just saying. You're not trained in law enforcement."

"Of course I'm not, because that's not what I do."

Wayne took a breath. "I just think that you're putting yourself in danger."

"I can take care of myself," Truman said, and waved a hand. "Maybe you're the one who's in the wrong job. Maybe you should be a career counselor, or a life coach."

Wayne swiveled toward him. "I feel like we got off on the wrong foot here."

"Then stop telling me what to do."

"Truman, I have to say, you strike me as a bit of a hothead."

"I'm actually not." He looked away and slurped

his drink. "For some reason you bring it out in me."

"It's kind of turning me on."

"So maybe we can cut the chitchat, and go to my place, and mess around."

Wayne laughed. "That, I can do. The drinks are expensive here."

Truman drained his tumbler and slid off the barstool.

Once they were upstairs and on the street, Wayne said, "Did you drive?"

"We can walk. It's only a few minutes."

"I have a car. I left it at a meter." He gestured up the block, and Truman walked with him, matching his deliberate stride.

Wayne stepped into the street behind a vehicle and pressed his key fob. Its park lights flickered, and Truman looked over the dark SUV, then climbed in the passenger door. The vehicle was suspiciously bland, with nothing personal on the dash or in the backseat. He opened the glovebox and saw there was nothing inside.

"This car is from the federal motor pool," he said.

"Do you have a problem with that?" Wayne checked his side mirror and pulled into the street.

"Is some bureaucrat somewhere going to open a file on me when they see it was parked in front of my place?"

"You think your cell carrier and all the apps

on your phone aren't already doing that? The feds are way behind in terms of surveillance tech. The private sector compiles extensive records on you. What you really should be worried about is that lots of that data about you is sent overseas. What's the Chinese military doing with it?"

Truman directed him to his loft, pointing out an open meter in front of his building. He felt a little buzzed. Not walking home meant the tequila hadn't had the chance to burn off.

"You live in such a seedy neighborhood," Wayne said, surveying the street through the windshield. "Is one of these homeless people going to steal my ride?"

"What do you care? It's not really yours."

When they climbed out, Beretta appeared, ambling over from the alley.

"Hey, Sunshine," he said. "Do you need security tonight?"

"This particular car belongs to your Uncle Sam," Truman said. "So I'm not going to pay anyone to protect it."

"I understand," Beretta said, and gave Wayne the once-over. "Why would you defend that guy's stuff? He doesn't give a shit whether you live or die."

He walked back toward the alley, and Truman went to his front door.

"Why would you tell a homeless guy that it's

a government vehicle?" Wayne demanded.

"He's a friend of mine. He won't lay a finger on it. He sleeps outside, right, so he's not going to risk invoking the black helicopters and the searchlights and the storm troopers." Truman led the way up the stairs to his loft.

"You don't have a very high opinion of the federal government. I don't think your neighbor does either."

"It's nothing personal," Truman said. "I do pay my taxes."

Once they were inside, and he'd closed the door, he stepped closer to Wayne, and slid his hands inside his jacket, and leaned in to mouth his neck. Wayne took a breath, and tilted his head back. Truman could feel the tension draining out of his muscles, his breaths deepening as he started to relax. The guy was into this for real, he decided. It wasn't just a feint to interrogate him.

Wayne pulled his jacket off and draped it on the nearest sofa, then ran his hands over Truman's torso, and under his shirt. Once they both had their shirts off, Truman caressed his pecs, and Wayne grabbed his waist and pulled him closer, and ground his woody into him.

"This way," Truman said, and led him toward his bed.

"This place is huge."

"It definitely provides room to think. The

downside is that it's impossible to heat in the winter."

He ditched his trousers, and Wayne did the same, and climbed up, straddling him. Truman squeezed his cock.

"So where's your gun?"

Wayne chuckled, and nuzzled his ear and his hair. "If you mean my weapon, it's in a secure location, on a need-to-know basis."

"I bet it's in a gun safe in the back of that fleet vehicle."

He pulled back and met Truman's gaze. "You really could be a detective."

"I am a detective, you dick. I'm good at it too."

"Simmer down," Wayne said, massaging his chest.

"Do you say that to all the crooks?"

"We actually call them 'perps.'"

Truman pushed him onto his side, then climbed up and straddled him, pressing his hard cock into his belly.

"Such a hothead," Wayne said, ruffling his hair. "Do you want to fuck me like a hothead?"

Reaching for the bedside table, Truman grabbed a condom, and rolled it on, and soon was inside him, then pounding him. Wayne gasped with the intensity of it, holding Truman's gaze. Arching his back, Truman climaxed. Afterward, he met Wayne's mouth and stroked him until he came too, then flopped on his back to catch his breath. He was drifting toward sleep when Wayne spoke.

"I wonder if your friend in the alley figured out that there might be a weapon in my vehicle."

"Beretta? He's a veteran, so he might know about stuff like that."

"The guy is named after a gun?"

"I think it's a street name. I'm sure his mother didn't put that on his birth certificate."

Wayne shifted to meet his gaze. "I figured."

Truman caressed his belly, and they lay there quietly for a while.

Eventually Wayne said, "I should go."

"Are you worried about your car?"

"I have an early morning." He met his mouth, and spent a moment in it, then sat up and got dressed.

Truman got up too and walked him to the door. "Thanks for not interrogating me about Davo Avakian."

"That's business," Wayne said, and grinned. "This wasn't."

FIFTEEN

I**N THE MORNING, AFTER** Truman made coffee, he pulled open his computer. It felt like it was time to decide what Rolán was really up to. The guy should have called him back by now, to explain the discrepancy between his story and Davo's. But not responding, not providing any explanation, that in itself was informative.

Davo didn't seem like a blackmailer. His focus was on the weightier and significantly less petty project of trying to ship his money out of the country. Wayne was interested in Davo for that reason—his politics, not about any small-time local criminal activity.

Stretching out on the sofa with his computer and a cup of espresso, Truman researched hit-and-run incidents that involved pedestrians.

There were a lot of them, happening almost every day, far more than he expected. Most involved cars, and sometimes big trucks, but a few were about motorcycles.

One incident described on the police blog seemed to line up with what Rolán had told him. It had happened in Westmont, late at night, a few weeks ago. Witnesses said a transient had been sideswiped by a motorcycle, and he'd hit his head on the curb. The paramedics declared him DRT—dead right there. Truman saved a link to the article, then gazed out the windows at the daylit sky.

It was so close to Rolán's story. Was there any truth in it? Yesterday Davo said he wasn't a motorcycle guy, but that could be a lie. In the *Hard-Nosed Detective* book, Biff Sturgis said you had to assume everyone was lying, all the time, about everything. The only way to piece together the truth was to compare all the stories and find the parts that overlapped, the parts of it that different people told the same way. "The truth is immutable, and beautiful, and constant," Biff said. "It doesn't change, and informants don't have to think too hard to remember it."

So far, Davo's and Mariam's stories had no contradictions, but Rolán's had several. Truman folded his computer closed. Rolán was lying to him, he was sure of that now. He should have gone with his gut from the beginning—it had felt wrong, the way Rolán told the story. It was so hard to tell when people were lying to your face. The question now was, if Rolán was playing him, what was he really after?

Pulling out his phone, Truman dialed Davo's number.

"What do you have for me?" Davo said when he picked up.

"Can I drop by your warehouse today?"

"You know where to find me."

Once he was dressed, Truman pulled on his backpack, and set off for the metro, and rode to Vernon, where he walked through the industrial neighborhood. When he stepped inside Davo's business, Lina was at her desk.

"You're here for Davo?" she said. "Let me fetch him."

She rose and pushed her way through one of the doors at the back of the office. Truman caught a glimpse of the warehouse space beyond.

When Davo followed her back out, he flashed an easy smile, and greeted him with that booming voice.

"Truman. Come into my office."

Davo closed the door behind them, and sat across from him on the cramped blue club chairs.

"You have some ideas for me," Davo said.

"Not specifically about shipping," Truman

said. "Not yet. I want you to hire me. That way we'll have a confidential business relationship. I don't care what you're shipping, but if I can see it, maybe I can get some ideas about how to disguise it."

Davo sat back. "The problem I have with that is, I don't know you. You seem pleasant enough. But I've had trouble with employees before."

"I don't want to be your employee. Hire me as a contractor."

His brow furrowed, and he absently rubbed the back of his neck. "I know that Mariam thinks you're OK."

"To be fair, Mariam doesn't know me either."

"But she knows where you live, and she knows your fiancée. 'He's lucky he's getting married because the guy has no taste,' she said. 'His apartment looks like the alley behind a thrift store on trash day.' Your fiancée is the one with style, she said."

Truman could feel his cheeks burning. It seemed like a harsh assessment, especially from a woman who wanted to make his loft look like a field hospital on an ice rink.

Davo hesitated. "Do you really think seeing what I'm shipping will help you come up with a way to hide it?"

"I can't promise you anything, but I'll try. I've been going through the guidelines from Geneva."

"What's in Geneva?"

"The ISO."

"OK," he said evenly, and eyed Truman for a moment. Then he threw up his hands. "The world is full of crooks. Sometimes we just have to trust people." Davo rose and thrust out his hand.

Truman stood and grasped it, trying to match the power of his grip.

"Do you have time to work on this today? I need to get moving on it."

"Absolutely."

"So let's go for a drive."

He followed Davo out to the front office. "Where's the washroom?" he said, and when Davo pointed it out, he stepped in and quickly washed his hands. No way was he going to walk around all afternoon with Davo's germs on him if he didn't have to.

"I'll be back in an hour," Davo said to Lina, then waved for Truman to follow him out the front.

The green Bimmer was less roomy than he expected, considering the oversize engine wasn't even street-legal, but he pulled on his seat belt and got comfortable as Davo pulled onto the boulevard. He drove fast, and impatiently, changing lanes often to weave around the slow-moving freight trucks. Once they'd crossed the grungy LA River, he accelerated onto the 101.

"Are you not curious about where we're going?" Davo said, glancing over at him.

Truman knew exactly where they were headed, but he said, "I figured if you're putting your trust in me, I can at least trust you."

Davo laughed, his voice loud and deep. "That's good, Truman."

When he got off the freeway, he drove past the familiar high-rise self-storage building, and pulled into a fast-food joint at the end of the block. He parked in the narrow lot along the side and killed the engine.

They climbed out of the car, and Davo led him out to the sidewalk, then back toward the storage building. He paused at the keypad next to the pedestrian gate and punched in a code. The door clicked open, and they stepped through.

"This place has parking," Truman said, gesturing to the vehicle gate and the patch of striped asphalt. "Why did you park at the fast-food place?"

"There was an electrical malfunction with the gate. My car was stuck inside for hours. It was one of the first times I came here. I'm not going to take that chance again." Davo led the way into the building. "No one at the restaurant seems to mind."

Inside, he summoned the freight elevator, and they stepped on. Truman watched as he pressed the button marked 20 TO 39. After the slow ride up, Davo led him to unit 23, and unlocked it, and rolled up the door. Once he'd waved Truman in, he rolled it down again.

"Why do you need a storage unit," Truman said, "when you have a whole warehouse in Vernon?"

"These are sample pieces," Davo said, waving at the room. He stepped over to the tall dresser, and crouched, and pulled open the bottom drawer.

Hauling out one of the black canvas bags, he set it on a bar table that stood between them. Next he grabbed the other bag and put them side by side. Truman could hear the metallic crunch of the coins shifting inside. Davo stood with a hand on each bag, and held Truman's gaze.

"You can't talk about this to anyone."

"You have my word."

Davo tugged the zipper on one of the bags and pulled it open to reveal the coins. Truman stepped closer to gaze at the gleaming hoard.

"That's a lot of gold."

"This is what needs to go overseas," Davo said.

"I can see why it needs to be hidden." He took a breath. "It's all coins?"

"That's right. It weighs seventy pounds."

"So the shape of the container doesn't matter," Truman said. "And looking at these bags, I can see what the volume is."

"This gold is payment for armaments that have

been shipped to Armenian freedom fighters."

"You don't have to tell me what it's for."

"I want to explain," Davo said. "You need to know that it's a noble cause, and that I'm not a criminal." He picked up a coin and handed it to him.

"There's something about gold, isn't there?" Truman studied the coin, flipping it over in his fingers. "The way it catches the light. It's mesmerizing."

"It's also negotiable anywhere in the world. No bankers required."

Truman handed the coin back. "I understand you have a connection to Armenia. But you live here now. Why get involved in Old World problems?"

"Why do our tax dollars pay for our military to maintain bases in seventy other countries? And why do we fund NATO, and all those Middle Eastern wars? There are so many right now I can't even keep track of them all. Those are also Old World problems, wouldn't you say?"

Truman nodded. "I see your point."

"Armenia is personal for me," Davo said. "I have family and friends there. A century ago the Turks tried to kill my entire family, and every Armenian family. The aggression is still happening."

"So this is money that you owe someone,"

Truman said. "That means it needs to ship soon."

"The arms have already been delivered." He zipped the heavy bag shut. "It will be worth my life if I don't pay for them."

———◆———

ALONE AT HER DESK at the gallery, Celeste had the music turned up loud. Saffron wasn't here, and as usual there had been no walk-ins.

Truman stepped in the front door, a smile on his face. She reached for the keyboard and turned down the volume.

"Rock on," he said, and dropped into the chair across from her. "What kind of music is this?"

"It's called bolero. It's more from my parents' generation, but some local bands are reviving it."

"It's got a good beat, and you can dance to it."

Celeste threw up her hands. "And that's all that matters."

"So I went back to Davo's storage unit."

"Seriously?" She frowned. "Why?"

"Davo drove me there. I told him he had to show me whatever it was he wanted to ship, and he took me to see the coins."

"I can't believe he trusted you with that."

"He said Mariam likes us both. Especially you—she thinks I have no taste."

Celeste shook her head. "They are so lucky we're not chiselers."

"The point was to find out whether Davo was playing me. So far it doesn't look that way."

"How are you going to help him? You don't really know anything about packaging and shipping."

"He just wants some ideas," Truman said. "I can try, right?"

"Where are the coins going?"

"He didn't say, but he told me they're definitely a payment for supplying weaponry to some Armenian force."

"Mariam said he was in a political group," Celeste said. "It's probably the group's money, don't you think? Only part of it will be Davo's own funds."

"They're taxing themselves to help the homeland. I guess our taxes pay to arm people all over the world too."

Her eyes narrowed. "Do you even pay taxes?"

Truman laughed. "I pay plenty."

"So if Davo isn't lying, you think Rolán is."

"I know he is. Davo doesn't ride a motorcycle."

"At least he told you he doesn't."

"I think my instincts are pretty good."

"But you're not always right," Celeste said. "Remember that UFO quest? You read that book and then you ran around town getting freaked out that the Navy was surveilling you."

"That was a scary book. I'll admit it got a little

out of hand."

"So maybe you're wrong about Rolán."

"Maybe you've got a crush on him," Truman said, raising his eyebrows.

She gestured helplessly. "I'm trying to be objective."

"All Rolán talks about is breaking into Davo's house. Yesterday I told him that Davo denied having a motorcycle, and he hasn't even bothered to respond to that."

"So you think there's no helmet," Celeste said. "No blackmail."

"He might be blackmailing him with something else, but to me it feels like Davo has bigger stuff to worry about. He seems pretty much on the level."

"Mariam too." She folded her arms and leaned back. "Rolán's hit-and-run story didn't feel made up to me, though. Is that nuts?"

"It's hard to tell when people are lying to you. I did some digging, and I found a fatal-injury incident that fits with his story. A lot of the details are the same."

"You think it was him?" she demanded. "Rolán killed someone with his motorcycle?"

Truman shrugged. "It's possible, right? He had that story on the tip of his tongue."

"Maybe I should ask him."

"He'll never fess up to something like that."

"Do you know the time and the location of the accident?"

"Sure. There were witnesses. All the details were on the police blog."

"If Rolán uses location tracking on his phone," Celeste said, "maybe I could check whether he was there."

"That's such a good idea." Truman waved a hand. "I use that all the time to see where I've been. It's like part of my memory."

"Me too. But being the kind of guy he is, Rolán might not have it turned on. When you're acting shady, you don't want to create a record of it."

"I'll send you the article with the details." He pulled out his phone and tapped the screen. "How are you going to get into Rolán's phone?"

"I saw him unlock it the other night. I know his code. It was an easy one to remember."

He looked up and grinned. "You never know when you're going to need a bit of information like that."

"I think I was channeling you and that detective book when I noticed it. I could hear you quoting Biff Sturgis: 'Commit it to memory, toots.'" She sat up. "I'll see if Rolán is free tonight."

"Maybe you can squeeze in another hookup," Truman said, tucking his phone away.

"Is that all you think about?" Celeste demanded.

"How was Wayne, by the way?"

"He didn't stay long."

"Not the romantic type?"

"I think he was just curious about me," Truman said.

"Wayne thinks you're a seditious crook the way he thinks Davo is a seditious crook."

"Dude didn't even ask about Davo last night. He was just attracted to my natural charisma and hotness." Truman gestured widely. "It's understandable. I can't really turn it off."

"That sounds far-fetched. I bet he was really just assessing your criminality."

He raised his eyebrows. "In bed."

Celeste couldn't help but laugh at that.

WALKING HOME, TRUMAN THOUGHT about what Davo had said, about trusting him. Davo really had shared his secrets. It made him a little queasy—Truman didn't deserve his trust, as he was lying to him about almost everything. Their whole relationship was premised on Truman stalking the guy.

Right now he needed to read more about packaging and shipping, but first, when he got home, he grabbed the *Hard-Nosed Detective* book and stretched out on the sofa. Biff Sturgis's take on what he was feeling was unequivocal:

The daily grind of the detective can be dark. You'll have to break things, and lie all the time, and hurt people. It's all part of the process of becoming hard-nosed. If you're feeling guilty about that sucker you had to sap and left groaning in the gutter, or that dame you made love to over supper to get the goods and then dumped before dessert, remember that you have two options. One is to snap out of it and move on. The other is to look for another line of work.

———·———

"WHAT ARE YOU DOING tonight?" Celeste said, when Rolán answered the phone. She rolled her chair out from her desk and ran a hand into her hair, pushing it back.

"Seeing you, I hope."

"Do you want to eat out? I've been craving Chinese."

"You want to ride out to the SGV?" he said.

"I'm thinking old-school Chinese. As in Chinatown."

"Just tell me where and when."

After she gave him the name of a restaurant, and ended the call, Celeste sat staring across the gallery, a faint smile on her face. She was thinking about the plan she was concocting, how she was going to get her hands on his phone.

Her own phone buzzed, and she eyed the screen.

"Don't you have a cousin who works on cars?"

Truman said when she answered. "I met him at somebody's birthday."

"You probably mean Josué," Celeste said. "That would have been my dad's birthday."

"He's thin," Truman said, "with a mustache, and great hair, and smoking hot?"

"That describes several of my male relatives. But yes, that's the guy."

"His name is José?"

"'Ho-*sway*,' not 'ho-*zay*.' There's a *u* in there. It's a totally different saint."

"I kind of want to pick his brain."

"His shop is in Pico-Union," Celeste said. "Let me check to see if he's working today."

———◆———

A FEW MINUTES LATER Truman got the go-ahead from Celeste, along with the address of the garage where Josué worked. It was almost too far to walk, but maybe the warmth of the late afternoon sun would give him a chance to clear his head.

When he found the place, he stepped up to the open garage door, where a chubby guy in blue coveralls was leaning over the engine compartment of a pickup.

"I'm looking for Josué," Truman said.

The guy turned and shouted the name into the garage. A minute later, Josué appeared, wearing the same kind of blue coveralls. He was wiry, and had his dark hair tied behind his head.

"I remember you," he said, and smiled. "Celeste's not-boyfriend."

"That's exactly right."

"She said you wanted to talk about cars."

"Do you have a few minutes?" Truman said. "I could buy you a coffee."

"There's a *pupusería* around the corner. You can buy me a *pupusa*."

———◆———

As she was packing up, Celeste noticed a loose Ritalin tab in the bottom of her handbag, so she plucked it out and popped it. She didn't need it, of course, but it might give her better focus, and make her more engaging with Rolán.

It was interesting that he wanted to see her again after they'd slept together. His sister was back from her trip, he said, so they definitely wouldn't be going over there again. It meant that his motivation wasn't just about sex. That made the connection more tantalizing, and more difficult to sever if she needed to.

Once she'd locked up and set the gallery's alarm, she went out the back door to the alley. The golden light of the end of the day lit the tops of the buildings above the long shadows. Celeste climbed in her car and headed toward Chinatown.

SIXTEEN

AFTER HE'D TALKED TO Josué, and got some ideas about how engines work, Truman left him at his garage and walked up the boulevard. He sent Luis a text:

What time do you get off work?

His answer came a minute later:

Soon. Want me to swing by?

I'm out. Near Vermont and Pico. Close to your store.

I'll pick you up there in a few minutes.

Truman waited on the busy corner, leaning on the low cinder-block wall that bounded the parking lot, next to a wide stretch of sidewalk where some food vendors had set up. People bought tacos from a steaming table, and fruit from another cart. Eventually he saw the familiar maroon Pacer pull into the surface lot behind him. Truman stepped over the wall and walked toward it.

"Do you know this *panadería*?" Luis said, and gestured behind him as he got out of his car. "They have the best vegan cupcakes ever."

"A vegan bakery?" Truman said. "Around here?"

"Whoa, son—your Anglo biases are showing."

"It's not a bias. It just doesn't fit. This is a low-income immigrant neighborhood. Vegan stuff usually costs a premium."

"That's only true in white neighborhoods."

"I guess that makes me an uninformed privileged ass," Truman said, and waved impatiently. "Let's get some damn cupcakes and take them to my place."

Luis laughed and put his hand on Truman's shoulder as they walked over to the shop.

———•———

CELESTE FOUND AN OPEN meter along the row of old Cantonese restaurants. As she walked toward the place, she saw a motorcycle parked out front, with a black helmet lashed on the side. It looked like Rolán's.

Walking in, the decor hadn't changed much

since the 1940s. Broad round tables in the middle of the room were flanked by booths with vinyl banquettes. The place was only half full, and Rolán was already here, sitting at a booth. She slid in across from him, and he half rose, leaning across to kiss her.

"You look great," he said, beaming at her.

"Back at you."

His phone was sitting facedown on the table, she saw as she got settled, and he'd draped his leather jacket over the back of the seat.

"Do you know what you want?" she said.

"If we're sharing, you can just order."

The server stepped over, and Celeste asked her for tea, and ordered string beans in brown sauce, and a mushroom dish, and one with tofu.

"A woman who knows what she wants," Rolán said, once they were alone again.

"When it comes to Cantonese food, anyway."

The teapot arrived, and Celeste poured a cup for him, then for herself.

"So have you talked to Truman lately?" she said.

"I've kind of given up on that *pendejo*. He hasn't learned anything useful."

"He talked to Davo for you. Both of us spent time in his house. There was no sign of a motorcycle helmet."

His eyebrows shot up. "You went out there

too? I didn't know you were that involved. He took you with him?"

"The point is that Truman is working on it, not just sitting on his butt."

"Tell me about Davo's place," Rolán said. "There's no alarm, is there?"

The first dishes arrived, steaming mushrooms with veggies along with a pot of rice.

"How about you tell me about the helmet?" Celeste said, spooning rice onto her plate. "Davo says he doesn't ride."

Rolán avoided her gaze, his brow furrowing as he scraped mushrooms onto his own plate.

"Here's the thing," he said. "Davo didn't actually borrow my helmet. I was just mad at him for firing me."

She stared at him. "So you sent Truman on a snipe hunt."

"At first, maybe." He gestured with his chopsticks. "Then I wanted him to tell me about Davo's house."

"Why are you so interested in that?" she demanded.

"I don't want to lie to you."

"So don't."

Rolán paused to finish a mouthful of food before he spoke. "Davo does have something of mine that I want to get back."

"If Truman doesn't know what it really is,

how could he possibly help you?"

She watched him, and saw the wheels turning as he ate, considering what to say. That was rarely a good sign—it meant he was concocting more baloney.

The server returned with another dish, the string beans in brown sauce. Celeste moved the other plates so that she could set it down near Rolán's plate before she stepped away.

The table was crowded now, and the beans were right at the edge. This was her opportunity. Reaching for the rack of sauces at the side of the table, Celeste leaned forward and surreptitiously shoved her plate with her other hand. It sent the plate of string beans off the edge of the table, into Rolán's lap.

Rolán jumped up, inadvertently spilling his tea. "Jesus fucking Christ," he shouted.

"Oh, god," Celeste said. "Did it burn you?"

He had brown sauce all over the front of his jeans, she saw as he stood up, scattering beans onto the floor.

"It's not that hot," he said, "but what a damn mess."

"Go sponge off in the men's room," she said, and gestured toward the back of the restaurant. "I'm so sorry."

Rolán stepped away, focused on his pants, and as she'd hoped, he left his phone on the table.

The server hustled over with a cloth in hand.

"Can I get another order of the beans?" Celeste said, and slid toward the wall, out of her way.

A busboy came over to help clean up the mess. Celeste grabbed Rolán's phone and tried the unlock code she'd seen him use, 1595. It worked, and she opened the map software, and hurriedly found his timeline. Rolán did use location tracking, it seemed, and she tapped the date that the police blog said the motorcycle hit-and-run had happened.

The map showed a convoluted green line for that day. Rolán had been all over the place. When she zoomed in on Westmont, the tracking line ran right through the neighborhood, on the boulevard where the pedestrian had been run down. The markers nearest the site said he'd been there at 1:31 a.m. and at 1:33 a.m. She could feel her heart pounding. That's exactly when the incident had happened. It was Rolán. He'd hit somebody. The way he'd used the story, and spun it into a lie, and blamed it on Davo for his own purposes—it was callous, and remorseless.

She closed the app and pressed the power key to kill the screen, then set the phone back on the table. The busboy was finishing his cleanup, and the server set down another order of the beans, making sure it wasn't near the edge of the table. When Rolán came back, the front of his jeans was wet, but at least the brown sauce was gone.

"I'm an idiot," Celeste said, watching him sit down.

"It's no big deal," he said, and grinned.

Celeste watched as he loaded more food onto his plate and tucked in. She wasn't an idiot for spilling the dish; that had been intentional. She was an idiot for believing anything this guy said.

TWILIGHT WAS FADING WHEN Luis parked in front of Truman's loft.

"Do you think your homeless friend is around?"

"You've been here before," Truman said, and popped the door handle. "If he sees your ride, he'll make the assumption it's covered, and hit me up later for the security fees."

"That's quite the alternative economy they're running." Luis lifted the pink pastry box of cupcakes from the back seat and climbed out.

"I can't fault them. Nobody at any level of government seems to be willing to change things."

Once they were upstairs in his loft, Luis handed Truman the pastry box and went into the bathroom. When he came back, he put his hands on Truman's waist, and mouthed his neck. His skin was so warm, his mouth so intent. Truman pulled him closer, so he could feel his wood, and ran his hands into his hair.

WHEN THEY LEFT THE restaurant, after Celeste had seriously overtipped to compensate for the mess she'd made, they stood on the sidewalk out front. Rolán pulled on his jacket.

"How are you pants?" she said.

"I'm almost dried out." He grinned. "I wish we could go somewhere, and spend some time alone."

"That's the curse of living with your family."

"I suppose your parents wouldn't approve of you having a visitor."

"It wouldn't work," Celeste said. "It's a small house."

"I know how it is. Maybe we could make out in your car."

"Right here? On the street? No way."

"It's quiet enough," he said, and looked around. "This is basically a backstreet, and it's in the middle of nowhere."

"It's Chinatown, Rolán," she said flatly. "We're going to have to call it a night."

AFTER THEY HAD SEX, and Truman drifted into sleep, Luis got out of bed and walked over to the kitchen counter.

"What did you do with the cupcakes?" he called across the room.

Truman woke up and shifted to look at him. "Sir, the cupcakes are in a secure location, on a need-to-know basis."

"I actually need to know."

He got up and took the pastry box out of the pantry cupboard. Each of them ate one, and as they stood at the kitchen counter, Truman admired Luis's naked form. He wasn't muscly, really, just effortlessly buff. Watching him devour the little cake, he had to smile at Luis's earnest approach—the methodical way he peeled off the paper, the way he bit into it. Besides the physical attraction, he liked his demeanor, how he stood up to Truman, and challenged him without softening it. The guy was easy to be around.

"So what's Rolán's deal?" Truman said. "He hired me to find his spare motorcycle helmet. It turns out there isn't one."

"How do you know that?"

"I figured it out."

"I think he hired you to get him access to his boss's house."

"He never told me that. I can't help him if he's lying to me."

Luis peeled the paper from a second cupcake. "If he told you the truth, you probably wouldn't have agreed to help him."

"What is the truth?" Truman demanded.

"I don't know, exactly. He said Davo has more

money than god."

"He has more than Rolán or you or me, maybe, but he's not a one-percenter."

"I think Rolán saw something in his house." Luis paused to take a bite of his cupcake. "He said it was like El Dorado up there."

"What did he see?"

"I don't know. But it must be something that's easy to sell."

"You're saying that he wants to rob the guy."

"Of course not. But where we grew up, things were tough. You can understand the temptation. Lots of our friends wouldn't hesitate to do something like that."

Truman folded his arms, and pressed his mouth into a tight line. At least now he knew what Rolán was really after.

"Don't get steamed," Luis said. "You didn't do anything wrong."

"That's not the point."

"You've got frosting right here," Luis said, and tapped his own face.

"What are you going to do about it?" he demanded, and threw up his hands.

Luis chuckled, and stepped closer, and mouthed his upper lip.

SEVENTEEN

IN THE MORNING TRUMAN woke to the buzzer on the front door. He hopped out of bed and hustled over to the box. Luis was gone, he realized.

Celeste's voice came through the crackle of static, and he buzzed her in, and made sure the deadbolt was open, then hustled over to his clothes rack and stepped into a pair of sweatpants. He was pulling on a T-shirt when she walked in.

"Did I wake you?" Celeste said.

"I've been up for a while."

"Since I rang your bell, at least."

"Do you want a coffee?"

Truman padded over to the espresso machine to get it working.

"So I got into Rolán's phone." She stood nearby, watching him work, and folded her arms.

"Could you see his location history?"

"He was definitely in Westmont that night. The map shows that he rode through the accident site at exactly the same time."

"So it was him," Truman said, glancing at her as he poured them each a cup of java.

"It seems that way." Celeste took one of the cups and carried it to the sofas. "The other possibility is that he was with another biker, and maybe he just saw it happen. That's why he knows about it."

Sitting across from her, Truman sipped from his cup and thought it through. "The article on the police blog said the witness saw a motorcycle. There was no mention of a second motorcycle, or a passenger on the back, or anything like that."

"So it's not likely." She sipped her coffee. "Either way, perp or witness, Rolán was there."

"Last night Luis basically admitted that Rolán's plan all along has been to rob Davo. That's why he's so focused on his house."

"You said the safe was empty," Celeste said. "Does he want the silverware or something?"

"I think he knows about the coins, and he thinks they're in that house. He said something to Luis about El Dorado."

"The golden city."

"The mythical golden city," Truman said. "It's not at Davo's house."

Celeste sighed. "He's so hot. Why do we get mixed up with so many lowlifes?"

"It pisses me off that he's been playing me all along. I want to slap him silly."

"Is that a Biff expression?"

"How did you know that?" Truman said, and frowned.

"It's not something you hear much in this century. In my neighborhood they'd just say, 'I want to bust a cap in his ass.'"

"That would give the wrong impression— that I carry a firearm."

"It's probably best not to escalate," Celeste said. "Stick with the slapping. So what's next?"

"I'm going to ask Rolán to pay me."

"He's never going to do that."

"I have to ask. It means I can finalize things, and tell him I know he's been lying to me."

"Good luck," Celeste said, and stood up. "I should get to work."

"Are you going to see Rolán again?"

"He's a lowlife," she said, and shrugged. "I'd rather focus my energy on guys who aren't."

After she left, Truman called Rolán, and left a message on his voice mail: "We need to talk."

Once he'd made another pot of espresso, he sat on one of the sofas with his computer, reading more about some of the stuff he and Josué had talked about. Eventually he had everything straight in his mind, and he called Davo to make sure he'd be at his warehouse.

Once Truman had changed into street clothes—a pair of chinos and a buttoned shirt—he slung on his backpack, and set off for the metro, and walked from the train to Davo's place in Vernon. A powder-blue shipping container on a flat trailer was parked beside the building, backed in to one of the loading docks. Its doors were folded open, and in the gap between it and the loading bay door he could see a couple of guys carrying a bulky object, tightly wrapped in plastic, into the warehouse. He couldn't tell what it was, but it didn't look heavy—likely more rattan furniture.

When he stepped into the front office, Lina looked up and smiled in recognition. She summoned Davo, and he stepped out of his office, and greeted Truman with his usual loud bluster.

"Can we step outside?" Truman said.

Davo frowned. "Why?"

Truman waved for him to follow, and walked out to where the cars were parked.

"Do you know Salt Lake Park?" Truman said. "It's really close to here. Down at Florence."

"You want to go to the park?"

"So we can talk privately."

Davo grinned and waved toward the office.

"You think Lina is listening in?"

"I'll explain, but not here."

"If you insist," Davo said, stepping over to the Bimmer. "I can drive, but I've never heard of this park. You'll have to direct me."

Once he'd pulled into the street, he spoke again.

"We can't even talk in my car?"

"I'm not sure," Truman said, "so let's wait."

A few minutes' drive brought them to the park's asphalt surface lot. People were playing soccer on the lawn on the far side, but it was quiet here. Truman climbed out and walked over to a picnic bench among the trees. Davo followed him over, and dusted off the bench, and sat across from him.

"Why all the mystery?" Davo demanded.

"First, let me tell you about my research."

"You have an idea for me?"

"Do you know what a two-stroke engine is?"

"Maybe." He spread his hands. "Refresh my memory."

"It's the gas engines on lawnmowers and small motorcycles," Truman said. "Usually they're really noisy compared to a bigger and more complicated engine, like in a car."

Davo nodded. "OK."

"They have big piston chambers. Much bigger than in a four-stroke engine. You might be able to do it yourself, or you could get a mechanic to take off the top part of the engine—it's called the head—and then take out the pistons. That would leave lots of room to put your cargo inside. Bolt the head on again, and the extra weight won't be noticed. Those little engines are heavy."

A smile spread on Davo's face.

"A two-stroke engine is hard to start," Truman said. "Not like a car engine. You need a pull-cord. I'm thinking no middleman or customs person is going to try to start the engine, or open it up. Who wants a puddle of crankcase oil on the floor?"

Davo laughed. "I get it, Truman."

"You should be able to buy them at a junk-yard." He gestured vaguely. "I don't know where you're sending your payment. If you're shipping it to Switzerland or France, a customs officer might find it a little strange to see cheap used engines from California. But in a less developed country like Armenia, it wouldn't be surprising that they'd need things like that."

"This is a brilliant idea."

Truman nodded. "Make sure you pack the coins tightly so that the payload doesn't rattle around."

"I can handle all that." He threw his hands up. "This is why I hired you. I knew you'd find an answer for me."

"I hope it works."

"I know it will work. I can make it work." He waved a hand. "What do I owe you for this research?"

"I didn't really do much. How about five hundred bucks?"

"Done. Now, explain to me why we're sitting in a park."

Truman shifted uncomfortably. "A DHS agent has been sniffing around."

Davo frowned. "Did you talk to him?"

"I told him that I hired your wife to decorate my loft. That's not why they're interested in you."

"I'm not afraid of them," he said. "I'm not doing anything wrong."

"Wrong and illegal don't always line up. This guy somehow knew that you and I and Celeste and Mariam are connected. That means either someone in your circle is talking to them, or more likely, the feds are monitoring you."

"Damn it," he snapped.

"I think you just have to take some basic precautions so that they don't find out about your coins. Don't use your phone or email to discuss the shipment. Maybe use someone else's computer to get a new email, or buy a prepaid cell phone. You don't have to let them monitor you."

"I know exactly why they're interested in me," Davo said. "It's my political activities. They came to my warehouse unannounced a few weeks ago. A whole group of them. They went through everything. I know they were looking for weapons." He scoffed. "As if I'd source them in this country."

"They had a search warrant?"

"My lawyer said it was one of those secret court documents that they use to go after terrorists." He raised his voice. "I'm not a terrorist."

"Celeste did some research about what's happening in Armenia. I know you're not doing anything wrong. But we live in strange times."

"Don't tell the Zepo anything," he said sharply.

"The Zepo?"

"It means the secret police. The DHS or the FISA court or whoever is stalking me."

"I can't tell them anything," Truman said, "because I don't know anything. Except that Mariam is decorating my loft, and you showed me some rattan pieces at your warehouse, and we came to the park today to get some sunshine and talk about furniture."

Davo eyed him for a moment, still scowling, but then cracked a smile. "I don't know why I trust you, but I do. Maybe it's because you're soft."

"I might look soft, but I'm not a pushover."

"I know you're not stupid." Davo shrugged. "If you had informed on me, the Zepo would have already searched my storage unit."

"It's none of my business what you do with your money. Personally I don't think it's any of Uncle Sam's business either."

He scoffed and stood up. "That's not how they see it."

AFTER DAVO DROPPED HIM at the metro station, as Truman waited on the platform, just as he saw the train approaching, his phone buzzed. It was a text from Rolán:

You around now?

Finally, Truman thought. He texted back:

I'll be home in half an hour.

Not long after Truman got upstairs to his loft, his phone rang. It was Mariam. Most likely she'd be intent on sending her crew over here to measure the place. He let it go to voice mail.

As he tucked his phone away, Rolán buzzed the front door. When he stepped inside, he was wearing his leather jacket, and had his helmet in hand.

"Do you want a coffee or something?" Truman said.

"No, man." He gestured impatiently. "What have you got for me?"

Truman decided not to ask him to sit, and

instead stood there by the door, facing him.

"Well, I know that Davo doesn't have your other helmet."

He jutted his chin. "Celeste told you."

"I figured it out on my own. Davo doesn't ride."

"What did you tell him?" Rolán demanded.

Truman put his hands on his hips. "Nothing about you, because you're supposed to be my client. But you've been playing me all along. Lying to me about what you really wanted. It's time for you and me to wind things up."

"So you've got nothing."

"I've got an invoice for you. Let's call it twenty-five hundred."

Rolán laughed. "I'm not going to pay you anything. Mostly because you didn't tell me anything useful, but also because you're stupid."

"Fuck you," Truman snapped.

"You fucked yourself." His lip curled into a sneer. "It was stupid of you not to get the money up front. Who does business like that? I know you're no detective. You're really just a tour guide. A carless fool playing dress-up."

"Get out of my place," Truman demanded, and pointed at the door.

Rolán raised his eyebrows, and shifted his weight. It was a tacit challenge, to emphasize pointedly that he had the physical advantage, that there was nothing Truman could do to make him move. After a moment he turned toward the door.

"Bye, sucker."

When he stepped out, Truman flipped the deadbolt behind him, and took a deep breath. It had gone down about the way he'd expected, without any money changing hands. A moment later he heard the sputter of a motorcycle engine as it started up, and the roar of it pulling away.

Biff Sturgis said a hard-nosed detective's loyalty was always to the client. In the book he quoted an old song: "I'll dance with the one that brung me." Biff meant that you didn't switch allegiance just because someone else offered to pay you more. But that was no longer an issue. Truman was finished worrying about Rolán's interests—he was absolved of any loyalty to the guy.

———•———

PULLING ON HIS BACKPACK, Truman walked over to Celeste's gallery. As he stepped inside he glanced up at the dark offices on the mezzanine.

"Saffron's not here," Celeste said, leaning back in her chair. "She might come in later."

"So I'm officially done with Rolán," he said, dropping into one of the chairs in front of her desk.

"Did he pay you?"

"Of course not. He called me stupid to my

face." He told her about Rolán's visit, and his earlier meeting with Davo.

"I can't believe the feds searched Davo's warehouse," Celeste said.

"Wayne told us why. They don't want him arming somebody else's combatants."

"And yet we're supposed to be on board with our tax dollars bankrolling a bunch of Arab despots' wars because they have all that oil. I say to hell with Wayne."

"Agreed," Truman said. "The question is, what do we do about Rolán?"

"You just said you were done with him." She waved a hand. "He lied to both of us, and trash-talked you to your face. I'm done with him too."

"He probably killed a guy."

"So you want to turn him in."

He shrugged. "Is that the right thing?"

"What good would it do?" Celeste said. "It wasn't intentional, and whether he gets busted or not, the victim is still going to be dead."

Truman nodded and got up. "I guess all that's left is to get Davo to pay me."

"You should have got the money up front."

"I know. I'm stupid that way."

———•———

ON THE WALK BACK to his neighborhood, Truman's phone buzzed in his pants pocket. He didn't recognize the number, but he answered anyway: "Boudreaux."

"It's me," Davo said.

"You got another phone."

"Listen, buddy—can you meet me at that place we went yesterday?"

"Is it about the engines?" Truman said. "I'm not really good at that kind of work. Mechanical stuff, and tools. I don't really want to get my hands dirty."

"Don't worry about that. I've got some money for you."

"I'm already out doing stuff. I can be there in half an hour."

"Turn your phone off before you come," Davo said. "If they're tracking me, they could be tracking you."

That didn't seem likely, he thought, after he'd ended the call. Maybe Davo was being a little paranoid. But Truman had planted the seed, when he'd taken him to that park, and it couldn't hurt to be too careful. He crossed the street and headed toward the metro.

EIGHTEEN

AT HER DESK, CELESTE was absorbed in reading about a local artist, looking at her portfolio, when the front door swung open, revealing Wayne. He was wearing an officious dark suit and that same yellow necktie.

"What are you doing here?" Celeste said, leaning back in her chair. "I don't know anything more than I did on Monday."

"You and your friend are more involved that you said." Wayne pulled out one of the chairs in front of her desk and sat down, holding her gaze.

"Oh—would you like to have a seat?" Celeste said, gesturing at where he was already sitting.

"Your boyfriend went to see Davit Avakian this morning."

"He's not my boyfriend. Although from what

I've heard, you're in the running, what with the way you put out for him."

Wayne's expression didn't shift, but his face might have reddened a little.

"The two of them went directly to a park," Wayne said.

"I heard they had a picnic today. It's nice, right, that a straight guy can have lunch with another man without it being awkward."

"I think they were trying to avoid being overheard. It's a tactic that drug dealers use."

"Drugs?" she said, raising her eyebrows, her tone incredulous. "Truman wouldn't know junk from jellybeans. And if you know they went to a park, it just confirms that you're surveilling Davo. What did he do to upset you so much?"

"It's not personal. Like I said before—Americans aren't allowed to conduct their own foreign policy."

"Why are you coming to me with this? If you want to know what they had for lunch, you should talk to Truman." She raised her eyebrows. "Or is he not answering your calls? That must have been quite the tumultuous date."

"I'm giving you a chance to get ahead of this, Ms. De la Torre, and tell me what you know."

"I've already told you everything I know. Mariam and I work together, and Truman had lunch with Davo. If you want to lock me in a cage like a migrant preschooler, or waterboard me, or send me to Gitmo, lo—my answers will be the same."

Wayne sighed. "You're a tough one."

"And you're starting to get on my nerves. If you're not here to buy art, you can be on your way."

———◦———

WALKING EAST FROM THE metro line, in the long shadows of the early evening, Truman wondered how he was going to get into the self-storage place if he couldn't phone Davo. When he got there, though, he found that Davo must have foreseen the issue—the pedestrian gate was propped open by a short chunk of wood.

He rode the lumbering elevator up to the floor where Davo's storage was, and saw that the door to unit 23 was rolled half open. He knocked lightly on the steel shutter, then ducked underneath it.

Something was wrong—Truman saw it right away. Davo was here, standing in the space and facing him, but his eyes were hard.

"What's going on?" Truman said.

Davo stepped behind him and rolled the door all the way down, then reached behind his back, and pulled out a handgun, and leveled it at Truman's chest.

"Whoa," Truman said, instinctively flashing his palms. "Don't point that thing at me."

"Start talking," Davo demanded.

"About what?"

His heart was pounding, and he couldn't look away from the weapon, the cold metal, the ugly muzzle. At least the guy knew how to use it—his index finger was outside the trigger guard. That meant he was much less likely to shoot him unintentionally. But the bad news was that if he did fire, he wouldn't miss.

"Rolán Hernández," Davo said. "Do you know him? Don't lie to me."

"I do," Truman said carefully.

"Damn it," he snapped. "You're trying to steal from me."

"I'm not. Rolán might have that intention, but I'm not part of that."

Davo gestured with his free hand. "I was driving with Mariam today. She said, 'Oh, this is where that charming young couple is going to live, right in this neighborhood. Maybe Truman is home. I'll show you his place.' When we pulled up in front, to my great surprise, my former employee stepped out of your building and rode away on his motorcycle. Rolán, the guy who tried to steal from me. And he's a friend of Truman's."

"We're not friends. But I can see how that would look suspicious."

"Talk," Davo shouted.

"First, point that thing away from me."

He took a step back, and aimed the weapon slightly to the side. Truman took a deep breath.

"Before I met you, Rolán hired me. He told me you'd stolen something from him and that you were blackmailing him. So I started to look into you."

Davo frowned. "You were researching me? Like an investigator?"

"Yes," Truman said, and winced.

"I never blackmailed that deadbeat. What would be the point? He doesn't have anything that I want."

"I figured that out."

"What did he say that I stole from him?"

"A motorcycle helmet," Truman said. "I know now that Rolán was giving me a snow job."

"Ridiculous." Davo looked thoughtful, and then his eyes narrowed. "You did research about me, and my wife?" he demanded.

"Once I talked to you, I knew that you weren't the crook." He took another deep breath, trying to calm his pounding heart. "I think Rolán knows about your coins. He thinks they're at your house."

Davo was quiet for a moment, his brow furrowed. Still staring at Truman, he absently bit his lip.

"You didn't tell him where they really are," he

said finally. "If you had, he would have come here as soon as he knew."

"Rolán was using me," Truman said. "He was at my place today because I wanted to conclude our relationship. I told him I knew he was lying to me, and I asked him to pay me for the research I did."

"He would never pay you."

"You're right—he refused."

"I believe what you're telling me about Rolán," Davo said. "It fits with what I know. But what about the shipping industry? Is that a lie?"

"Can we call it an exaggeration?" Truman spread his palms. "I'm something of a renaissance man. A little information about lots of different things. I know something about shipping, even though it's not my primary job. The idea about the small engines will work. That's not a lie."

He scoffed. "My countrymen say, 'He knows many songs, but he cannot sing.'"

Reaching behind his back, Davo tucked the weapon into his belt. Truman lowered his hands and took a breath.

"I can't believe Rolán hired you," Davo said. "That guy was so lazy. In the warehouse he was a complete goldbrick. I don't know why I didn't fire him sooner."

"How did he find out about the coins?" Truman said.

"I had them in my office. In the warehouse. He got a glimpse of them. He wasn't supposed to, but he's the kind of guy who's always looking for an opportunity. Once he'd seen them, I knew they would never be safe there. That's why I moved them here."

Truman nodded. "He assumed you took them home."

"He had the nerve to try to break into my house. Last week Mariam's car was in the shop, so she took the BMW that day. Rolán thought no one was there. I saw him, and I knew what he wanted, and I chased him out of my yard. At least he was smart enough not to come back to work."

Truman did a neck roll, trying to dispel the adrenaline. For the first time he noticed there were three lawnmower engines on the floor, sitting on a moving blanket. They looked well used but they weren't rusty. Beside them sat a red toolbox, folded open, with a set of socket wrenches in the top tray.

"It looks like you won't have to worry about that stash for much longer."

———◆———

CELESTE WAS CLOSING UP the gallery when her phone buzzed. She dug it out to check—Truman.

"Are you leaving work soon?" he said. "I'm in

East Hollywood. Do you want to meet me at that Mexican place?"

"You sound stressed out."

"I am. I just had a gun pointed in my face."

"What?" she demanded.

"I'll tell you about it when you get here."

———◆———

IT WAS STILL EARLY enough that the restaurant wasn't that crowded, Truman saw, walking into the place. He got set up at a table and ordered guacamole and a couple of drinks. Before long Celeste appeared and sat across from him.

"I ordered you a margarita," he said. "They're so good here."

She clinked her glass on his and took a sip. "So who pulled a gun on you?"

Truman told her about the confrontation with Davo. "I thought he was going to put me in the meat house."

"Where?" Celeste said. "Is that another dust bowl expression from that detective book?"

"It means the morgue."

"At least Davo let you explain yourself before he capped you."

"He knew that if I'd wanted to steal from him, or help Rolán steal from him, it would have happened already." He slurped at his drink. "Plus I think he wanted to believe me."

"I also had a visitor today. Your detective book would call him a hot tomato. Tall, dark, carries a sidearm."

"Wayne?" Truman frowned. "What did he want?"

"He knew you went to a park with Davo."

"So they're tailing him."

"Or they have a tracker on his car," she said.

Truman thought about it. "That actually makes more sense. It's a lot less labor-intensive just to bug his phone and track his car. I should tell Davo about that."

"Can we order first?" Celeste waved at the server, and when she came over, they both asked for fajitas. Once the woman stepped away, she said, "If Wayne is tracking his car, the feds must know about the storage unit."

"I don't think so. When Davo took me there, he parked at a fast-food joint at the end of the block. He said he didn't want his car to be trapped by the faulty gate at the storage place."

"Maybe he knows he's being tracked? Either that or he's incredibly lucky."

"I want to call him," Truman said, "but there's a chance the feds are tapping you and me too right now. Can you borrow someone's phone?"

"Why can't you?"

"Because I'm not a hot woman."

Celeste grinned and dug her phone out of her

bag, then leaned toward a guy at a table a few feet away. He had scruffy brown hair and wore a plaid sport coat.

"I'm having trouble with my phone," she said, and waggled it. "Could I borrow yours for a minute? I just have to make a quick call."

"Is it to someone overseas?" the guy said, his brow furrowing.

Celeste tittered and flipped her hair with the back of her hand. "It's only across town."

"I guess that's OK," he said, and dug in his pocket.

"Do you want to hold mine as collateral?"

"I trust you," he said, and smiled.

Taking his phone, she dipped her chin, and met his gaze. "Thank you."

She really did know how to work it, Truman realized, watching the interaction. Celeste handed him the phone, then took a sip of her margarita. The guy frowned. Truman ignored him and looked up Davo's new number on his own phone, then dialed.

"It's Truman," he said, when Davo answered. "Somehow that Zepo guy knew we went to the park today."

"This is harassment," Davo shouted. "They're following me."

"I don't think so. If an agent was watching you, they'd know about that room we were in today. I think it's more likely that they have a tracker on your car. That's much cheaper and easier for them than sending a person to follow you."

"What does a tracker look like?" he demanded. "Where would they put it?"

"It must have a battery in it, right, so it can't be too small. They'd have to put it somewhere accessible, so it'll be on the outside. Check under the bumper, and in the wheel wells, and under the trunk."

"I'll look for it," Davo said. "If I find it, I'll smash it under my heel."

"Don't do that—they'll know you found it. Put it on another car. It'll take them a while to realize it's not you anymore."

"Truman, you're so good at this. I should hire you full-time."

"I was thinking you're really lucky that you don't park inside that place. You parked at a restaurant, so they probably thought you were having lunch. Even so, you should clear your stuff out of there."

"It's happening tomorrow afternoon, my friend. It's all arranged. I have a straw man set up to make the shipment, so my name won't be on anything. Soon there will be nothing left to find."

Truman ended the call, and handed the phone back to the guy at the next table.

"Thanks," he said flatly.

Truman focused on Celeste. "He didn't know about the tracker, but I don't think he was surprised."

———◆———

LATER, WHEN CELESTE WAS driving him back downtown, he texted Luis:

Are you around this evening?

His reply came a minute later:

It's not going to work, Truman. Lose my number.

"What the hell?" Truman said, rereading the message, not quite believing his eyes.

"What's going on?" Celeste said, glancing over at him as she braked for a red light.

"I think Luis just dumped me by text message."

"What did he say?"

Truman read the exchange to her.

"Do you think it's about Rolán?" she said.

"It has to be. Nothing else has changed since yesterday. What the hell did Rolán say to him?"

"You should ask him."

Truman thumb-typed another text:

What's going on?

"I think he blocked me," Truman said, staring at the screen.

"How can you tell?"

"All my previous messages get marked 'Delivered,' and then 'Read.' This last one has nada."

"Maybe his loyalty to Rolán precludes him from even talking to you," Celeste said. "If those two really are from gangland, that fits with the culture."

"I was into this guy." He tucked his phone away. "Listen, can you drop me at that hardware store in Westlake?"

"You're going to confront him at his work?"

"If he's done with me, he can damn well tell me to my face."

Celeste changed lanes, and altered her route, and eventually rolled up to the front entrance of the store. "Do you want me to wait?"

"The metro's right over there. I'll be fine."

Truman gave her an air kiss, then climbed out and walked inside. It took a minute of strolling the aisles to find Luis, but he was here, wearing his apron uniform and stacking cans of spray paint on a shelf.

Looking up as he approached, Luis scowled. "I'm working."

"You cut me off," Truman said, and waggled his phone at him. "Last night you were riding my dick, and tonight you block my number. At least you could explain that."

"There's no need to be crass."

"What's changed in the last day?"

"I know what you did to Rolán," he said, and jutted his chin.

"I didn't do anything to him. I told him he had to pay me for the work I did, and he laughed in my face."

"You went behind his back and talked to the guy he asked you to investigate. That's pretty trashy, Truman."

"Rolán was lying to me from the beginning. I only figured that out once I'd spoken to his former boss. And why should I have any loyalty to Rolán at all? He didn't pay me anything. That means he was never really my client."

"He's my lifelong friend," Luis said. "You really think I'd pick you over him?"

"It's not a competition. I thought you and I were having fun. That doesn't have to impact your relationship with Rolán."

Luis scoffed. "I knew this was a bad idea from the beginning. Getting involved with an entitled Anglo."

"What is it about me, specifically," Truman demanded, "that you think is entitled?"

"Do you suppose I could strut into somebody's workplace and confront them like this?"

"Yes, you could," Truman said, raising his voice, louder than he'd intended.

"Are you trying to get me fired?" Luis hissed,

and looked past his shoulder. "We're done, Truman. You need to accept that. Now, get out of here."

As he walked out, and headed toward the metro, Truman's heart was pounding, and there was a queasy lump in the pit of his stomach. In truth he hardly knew the guy, but dumping him out of some sense of loyalty to Rolán seemed completely irrational.

NINETEEN

I N THE MORNING, ONCE Truman had made coffee, he moved to the sofa and checked his phone. There was a message from Davo with a link to a video. When he clicked on it, the image was a black-and-white fish-eye view of the side of a building—Davo's house, he realized, with the familiar white Tudor stucco and the dark beams. Two windows were in view of the camera, with dark foliage at the other side of the frame. The time stamp said it was 3:20 a.m.

As he watched, a figure appeared from the corner of the house, wearing a leather biker jacket and black gloves. Even from a distance, and in profile, he recognized him instantly—it was Rolán. He pushed up on the sash, and when it didn't budge, he pulled a pry bar from the back of his belt and started to work it into the window frame.

At that moment a dog started to bark, muffled in the recording but throaty and unmistakable. Rolán turned away from the window, and hustled back the way he'd come, and the clip ended.

Truman pulled on a pair of chinos and a short-sleeved shirt, and went down to the street, and stepped into the alley.

"Yo, Beretta," he called, and waited.

Eventually the guy appeared, moving slowly, and strolled out to the sidewalk. His eyes were watery but he looked lucid.

"Good morning, Sunshine," he said. "You look especially lovely today."

"Thanks," Truman said, and frowned. "Have you got a cell phone?"

"I might have."

"Can I rent it? I need to make a short call. I'll give you a couple bucks."

"What's wrong with your phone?"

"I think my line might be tapped."

Beretta nodded. "I hear that a lot. Make it a fin and we have a deal."

He dug for the five, and palmed it, then passed it to him. It quickly disappeared into Beretta's pants, and he pulled out a flip phone, and handed it to Truman.

"I'll be right back." Truman walked over to

the front door to his building and sat on the steps, then dialed Davo's new number. "I saw that video," he said, when Davo picked up.

"What am I going to do about Rolán?" Davo demanded. "He was going to break in while we were sleeping. He's getting brazen."

"That guy is definitely persistent. At least your dog scared him away. Is that new? I didn't see it when I was there."

"I don't really have a dog. It's an electronic deterrent. Rolán will figure that out soon enough. Listen, Truman, he hired you. Maybe you can tell him to back off. Tell him there's no gold in my house."

"We're not really on speaking terms," Truman said, "but I might be able to come up with a way to handle him. Let me think about it. I'll call you later."

Rising, he walked back to the alley and gave Beretta his phone, then went upstairs. With his own phone, he sent Celeste a text:

We should talk. Rolán is escalating.

Her reply came a moment later:

I'm on my way to work. See you there.

Truman sent her a link to Davo's security video, then set off toward the Arts District. He should have worn a jacket, he realized, with the fall weather in the air. But he warmed up soon enough from the walk.

When he stepped into the gallery, Celeste was walking out of the workroom under the stairs. She had on a chic black-and-white dress under a red jacket.

"Did you find Luis last night?" she said, dropping into her desk chair.

Truman sat across from her. "He totally dumped me. It's some bro-code thing with Rolán. Plus he says I'm an entitled Anglo."

"I don't really see that. The privilege thing is built in, but you're aware of it, right, so you don't really exploit it, or act entitled."

He waved a hand. "It's fine. I hardly knew the guy. It's just that he was so foxy."

"We sure can pick them." She watched him for a moment. "I saw the security video. That's definitely Rolán."

"He's going to hurt somebody, don't you think?"

"He's got gold fever. Like Cortés and the conquistadors."

"That's kind of what I saw when I watched that video. The stubborn and dogged quest for gold."

"Is Davo going to call the cops?"

"I don't think he wants to attract that kind of attention right now," Truman said. "Not with

Wayne sniffing around, and the shipment he has to make. He wants me to handle it."

Celeste frowned. "How are you going to do that? You ended your business relationship with Rolán."

"I had some ideas as I was walking over here. I think I know how to handle Wayne as well."

"If we just ignore Wayne, he'll go away on his own," she said. "Like a paper cut, or a hangnail."

"I'm not sure that's true. If he came back to hassle you, it means he's still suspicious of us."

"And you think there's something we can do to change that."

Truman explained the kernel of an idea he'd come up with, and they debated the details, and finally settled on a plan. He dug out his phone and recited Wayne's number as Celeste dialed it on the gallery's landline.

"Truman and I have been talking," she told him when he picked up. "We decided we should come clean. We don't know a lot, but there's one piece of information that might be useful to you."

"Interesting," Wayne said. "Where are you?"

"I'm at the gallery right now, and so is Truman."

"I'll be there in a few minutes."

Celeste replaced the receiver and relayed Wayne's words.

"A few minutes?" he said. "Is he parked out

front or something?"

"The federal building is just a few minutes' drive."

"So let's get our story straight," Truman said, and they ran through it once more.

When Wayne stepped in, Celeste rose and greeted him. She knew that emulating his body language would subconsciously suggest that they were in accord, that she really was cooperating with him.

"Ms. De la Torre," Wayne said. "You look lovely. Truman, sharp as always."

"Back at you," Truman said.

Wayne eyed Celeste. "So what's changed since yesterday?"

"Can we sit?" she said, and pulled her chair close to her desk, then leaned on it and tented her fingers. "Yesterday you got me a little worried. I started to wonder if we'd inadvertently become involved with people that we didn't understand. People that we shouldn't trust. Truman decided to ask Davo why the feds were interested in him."

"Davo says you think he's a terrorist," Truman said.

Wayne scowled. "That's not true."

"But you did run a FISA-warrant search of his business," Celeste said, holding his gaze. "We don't want to get caught up in any part of anything like that."

"OK," he said evenly. "So what's the information you have for me?"

She eyed Truman. "Just tell him."

"Oh, god." Truman hesitated, eyeing them in turn, and took a deep breath. "So I'm riding in Davo's car. It's kind of messy, and I had to move some papers out of the way to sit down."

"When was this?" Wayne said, his brow furrowing.

"Yesterday. We had lunch. Anyway, the top sheet was a receipt for a unit at a self-storage place. It struck me as odd because the guy has a whole warehouse to store stuff in."

"Lots of people rent storage units," Celeste said, eyeing Wayne. "Maybe it doesn't mean anything. Do you have any idea how expensive those places are? It's like renting an apartment for your stuff."

Truman gestured helplessly, avoiding Wayne's gaze. "So I thought maybe what you were looking for in his warehouse—bazookas or rocket launchers or cruise missiles or whatever—maybe that stuff is in that storage unit."

Wayne was watching him intently. "Do you remember where this place was?"

"I made a note of it. I'm a detective, remember?"

He waved impatiently. "Where is it?"

"Have you got some paper?" he said, eyeing Celeste.

She handed him a notepad, and Truman leaned on the desk to write it down, and tore off the top sheet, and handed it to Wayne.

"Are you sure it's unit 23?" he said.

"I memorized it."

Wayne folded the sheet in half and stood up. "We'll have a look."

"Are you going to get a search warrant?" Celeste said.

"Sort of." He eyed her with a smirk. "Obviously you already know what a FISA warrant is. Those happen fast. No questions, no deliberating, no waiting."

Truman rose. "Don't shoot Davo."

"That won't be an issue. Davit isn't around."

"Why do you say that?"

His eyes narrowed. "Didn't he tell you?"

"We're not that close," Truman said. "The only thing we talk about is furniture. What happened to him?"

"Davit drove to Utah last night. He's still on the road." Wayne eyed them in turn, and gestured with the folded paper. "You're doing the right thing."

"I hope that's true," Celeste said quietly.

As Wayne walked out the door, he pulled out his phone. Truman stepped over to the glass and watched as he climbed in his vehicle, the familiar SUV from the federal motor pool, holding his phone to his ear. Once he'd driven away, Truman turned to Celeste, a broad grin on his face.

"Nailed it," she said, and held up a palm.

Truman slapped it and laughed. "Davo was smart to go to Utah."

"I suspect Davo was smart to find the tracker on his car and put it on a car with out-of-state plates, or a freight truck, or somebody's RV."

"At least the feds haven't figured that out yet. That strikes me as Wayne's downfall: he thinks he's smarter than the rest of us."

"He certainly was pleased with himself," Celeste said. "You know, the thing about Utah is actually informative. It means the feds don't have someone tailing Davo's car. It's just an electronic tracker."

"They're also not location-tracking his phone. I bet that's not in Utah."

"How long until they go into the storage unit?"

"I'd say Wayne is highly motivated," Truman said. "It took him no time to get here. I bet he's on his way over there now. That leaves trash-bag Rolán."

"The gold hunter."

"Conquistador of your pants."

"Stop that," she said flatly. "There might be a way to get him to quit bugging Davo that also keeps us insulated from it."

"Do tell," he said, and sat down again, and they spent some time debating the idea.

———·———

TRUMAN WAS STILL AT the gallery, parked in front of Celeste's desk, when his phone buzzed in his pants.

"It's your favorite G-man," he said, checking the screen. As he answered the call, he put it on speaker and set the phone on Celeste's desk.

"So I'm standing in this storage unit," Wayne said. "There's a lot of junk."

"Like what?"

"Well, there's one of those machines where you loop a canvas belt around your tush and it vibrates."

"You mean an exercise belt," Truman said. "I don't think those really work."

"I don't care whether it works or not."

"Seriously, though, think about it—have you ever seen one at your gym?"

Celeste covered her mouth, suppressing a laugh.

"There's also a tampon dispenser," Wayne said. "It only takes nickels."

"That seems way too cheap," Truman said. "It must be an antique."

"Christmas decorations, kid's clothes, kitchen junk. It's like a garage sale in here. Did Davit ever talk about any of this?"

"Not to me. None of it sounds familiar. I don't know what to tell you," Truman said. "That's the receipt I saw—Hollywood Storage in North Hollywood, unit 23. Can you tell me what it is that you're looking for?"

Wayne chuckled. "Later, Truman."

Once Truman ended the call, Celeste laughed out loud. "It seems that Wayne bought our sincerity."

"We were really sincere."

"I wonder how long he'll spend digging through that storage unit?"

"The longer, the better," Truman said. "With those dopes focused on NoHo, Davo might be able to move his shipment today without being harassed."

"Do you want to call him?"

"I'm sure he's busy. Should we make a plan with Mariam?"

Celeste nodded. "I'll call." She dug out her cell phone and dialed, happy that Mariam picked up. "Truman and I want to come up and see you. Will you be around later?"

"I'd love that," Mariam said. "Davo said he'd be home for dinner. Can we make it afterward?"

Once she'd ended the call, Celeste eyed Truman. "It's on."

"Pick me up later?" He stood up and stretched.

"We should take them something."

"That guy owes me money," Truman said. "I'm not going to give him anything. Plus there's the thing where he pulled a gun on me yesterday."

"Well, I'm doing business with Mariam. I'll take something."

"Luis showed me this great vegan bakery in Pico-Union. You could take cupcakes."

Celeste frowned. "There's a vegan bakery in that neighborhood?"

"When I asked that same question, Luis called me an entitled ass. It's actually a *panadería*. It seems things are changing over there."

TWENTY

A FEW HOURS LATER, CELESTE rang his front door, and Truman pressed the button to unlock it.

"I could have just come down," he said when she stepped in.

"I wanted to make sure you wore something decent."

"Good thinking." They walked over to his clothes rack, and he pulled out a clubbing shirt, an iridescent jumble of colors with a wide collar. "How's this?"

"See, this is why I had to come up. What would you wear to a business meeting?"

"It depends where it was."

Celeste waved a hand. "A lawyer's office."

Flicking through his shirts, he pulled out a

somber gray collared shirt.

"That's the one."

Once he'd changed, they went down to Celeste's little blue car, and Truman directed her to the *panadería*. It was still open, and they both went in, and walked out a minute later with six cupcakes in a pink pastry box.

Celeste navigated to the freeway, and they drove up into the hills, and onto Mulholland. Twilight was fading when they pulled into the driveway at Davo and Mariam's place. The Bimmer and the gold Lexus were both in front of the house, and Celeste parked next to them.

"Don't forget the cupcakes," she said, climbing out.

Truman chuckled. "That's all I've been thinking about the whole drive up here."

When they rang the bell, Davo pulled open the door, beaming at them. He was wearing jeans and a green golf shirt.

"Look at you two," he said, "dressed so nicely. It makes me happy just to see you. Come on in."

"I heard that you'd gone to Utah," Truman said, as they followed him into the foyer.

Davo guffawed, tossing his head back. "I'm glad someone thinks that."

Mariam appeared from the back of the house, wearing a leopard-print blouse and a black skirt.

"For you," Celeste said, and handed her the

pastry box. "It's cupcakes."

"Oh, you know the way to my heart," Mariam said.

She waved them into the sitting room, where a bottle of champagne sat in an ice bucket on the coffee table, along with four flutes.

"What's the occasion?" Celeste said, dropping onto the sofa.

Davo sat across from her. "It's to celebrate the completion of some business that Truman and I have been working on."

"Can I pour?" Mariam said. She shifted closer to the table and pulled the bottle out of the bucket. "It's French."

"That's good stuff," Celeste said, eyeing the label.

"I take it things went well today," Truman said to Davo.

"Very well." He glanced sidelong at Mariam. "Although you have no idea how expensive air freight is."

Truman grinned. "I guess it depends on what you're shipping."

"Let me just say that by tomorrow night, there's a village in the Caucasus Mountains that will receive several engines as backups to pump their water supply."

Mariam handed each of them a flute.

"Well, congrats on your philanthropy," Truman

said, and they all tapped their glasses.

"These are the things I don't want to know," Mariam said, once she'd had a sip. "Not in detail, anyway."

Truman tipped his glass toward her. "We call that plausible deniability."

"My thinking is that if he gets arrested, the Zepo won't be taking me with him."

"You're very pragmatic," Celeste said.

Mariam chuckled. "My grandmother used to say, if you make a cake, eat it now. If you wait, someone will take it from you."

"I know there's a long history of people trying to take your stuff."

"Doesn't that mean we should have the cupcakes now?" Truman said. "That's what I'm taking away from this conversation."

Celeste frowned. "Will that work with the champagne?"

"I'm willing to take that risk," he said, holding her gaze.

After they'd each eaten one, Truman eyed Davo. "I wonder if we could talk business for a minute."

"You want to get paid," Davo said. "I knew this day would come."

"It's actually about your late-night visitor."

Davo set down his flute, and rose, and waved for him to follow. They walked through the foyer into the other living room at the back of the house. Big windows faced the pool, glowing soft blue in the darkness, and Davo slid the glass door open. They stepped out onto the pool deck. The water undulated lazily, distorting the underwater lights.

"So what can we do about that goldbrick biker?" Davo said.

———◆———

CELESTE REFILLED MARIAM'S FLUTE, then her own.

"I have a bit of bad news," Celeste said. "We've decided we're not going to live in the loft. We're going to get a house or a condo instead."

Mariam's brow furrowed. "Oh—that's such a shame. I had big plans for that space. It's so dramatic."

"We can pay you for the consultation."

She gestured with her glass. "I'm not worried about that. You and I are going to make plenty of money together."

———◆———

ON THE POOL DECK, Truman slid his hands into his pockets.

"I was thinking you could give Rolán something else to worry about. It would take his focus off you."

"What are you talking about?"

"I'm pretty sure Rolán killed a guy with his motorcycle. It was a hit-and-run. You could turn him in—anonymously, even."

"How do you know this?"

Truman shrugged. "Research. You know how you can set your phone to keep track of where you've been? Rolán uses that, and the location history on his phone puts him at the scene of the accident. If I were going to turn him in, I'd tell the prosecutors to subpoena his location records. The evidence is there."

"Running away is a felony," Davo said. "Even if it was an accident, he has to face up to it. Getting arrested would definitely change his priorities. Tell me about what happened."

He dug out his phone. "This article has all the details. I'll forward it to you."

Davo spent a minute scanning it on his own screen. Eventually he looked up. "So what was Rolán supposed to pay you for stalking me?"

"It's not important," Truman said, and waved a hand. He felt his face heating up. "I knew I wouldn't get paid. It was a couple grand."

"I owe you five hundred for the shipping research, plus more for your help with the Zepo, and your research on this accident of Rolán's."

"Five hundred is fine."

Digging in the pocket of his jeans, Davo

produced a handful of gold coins. "I had a few of these left over."

"They didn't all fit inside the engines?"

"The price of gold changes every day. I didn't have to send them all."

He handed Truman three of them. Looking at them in his palm, even in the pale light from the pool, they gleamed in that marvelous way that only gold could.

"I know what these are worth," Truman said. "This is extremely generous. Are you sure?"

"Besides the work you did, part of it is an apology, for pointing a pistol at you. Part of it can be a wedding gift too. Use it for the honeymoon."

They walked back to the front room, and the four of them sat and talked for a while, and eventually Truman and Celeste said their good-byes.

As they climbed into her car, Truman said, "Take Crescent Heights. We'll get a drink at that place on Sunset."

Celeste flicked on her headlights. "So did you get paid?"

"Depending on what the price of gold is today, I made about six grand."

"He gave you coins." Celeste laughed, nosing the car onto the dark street. "Davo did seem pretty happy with you."

"With us. You did lots of legwork. We'll split the payout." He chuckled. "Davo said we should use it for our honeymoon."

"You came clean about most of what was going on, but I guess it was too difficult to back out of that lie once we'd invested in it."

"I didn't want to admit to lying to Mariam. She was having so much fun with the decorating."

"It's hard to believe that they both think we're a couple," Celeste said. "I'm surprised they didn't question why I'm not with a butch guy."

"Ouch," Truman said. "I guess your type is more like the biker felon."

"Maybe it's because lots of hot women have plain boring boyfriends. It basically guarantees loyalty. Like a tiny gray asteroid orbiting the brilliance of the sun."

"Your ego is definitely brilliant like the sun." He sighed. "So nobody bagged a boyfriend on this deal."

Celeste clicked her tongue. "This time the coins in your pocket make up for it."

———·———

Also from Dagmar Miura

The Margarita Solution

In the first novel in the Truman and Celeste series, Truman stumbles into a detective gig and Celeste works her contacts in the art world as they wrangle with a series of lowlifes and some toxic secrets.

truman.dagmarmiura.com

When the Contralto Sings

When Celeste runs into Angel, one of the city's multitudinous homeless population, she invites her and Truman to a street festival, where they get hired to track down some seemingly valueless stolen property. The duo subsequently uncover a hotbed of corruption.

celeste.dagmarmiura.com

The Slater Ibáñez Books

Don't mess with the hothead—or he might just mess with you. Slater is only interested in two kinds of guys: the ones he wants to punch, and the ones he sleeps with. Things get interesting when they start to overlap.

slater.dagmarmiura.com

The Mason Braithwaite Paranormal Mystery Series

No one is ever quite sure whether psychic investigator Mason gets results with actual psychic power or his more mundane flatfooting, but the disheveled redhead manages to resolve some intractable mysteries.

mason.dagmarmiura.com

The Hillside Roble

Investigating a million-dollar heist at a gallery in the Arts District, Slater can't get a face-to-face with the owner, Eli, until he applies a little pressure. Eli turns out to be a minor celebrity, physically flawless but obsessed with his own image, and flaky in that uniquely LA way.

slater.dagmarmiura.com

Penstock Canyon

While helping out a friend suffering from late-night visitations, psychic investigator Mason is confronted with aliens on the roof and other liminal beings that have him questioning the very nature of reality.

mason.dagmarmiura.com

For Position Only

In the second novel in the Truth, Lies and Love in Advertising series, Craig Keller, a wealthy Los Angeles advertising magnate, is forced to face his demons or lose the woman he loves.

adeleroyce.dagmarmiura.com

The Psychic Vegan Cookbook

It has never been easier to cook vegan, and you don't even need to be psychic to do it. Whether your motivation is eating healthier or the welfare of other sentient creatures, Henrietta Flores guides you through plant-based versions of familiar dishes.

cookbook.dagmarmiura.com

9 781951 130572